Dead on a Rifle

A Josephine Stuart Mystery

by
Joyce Oroz

For information, email Cozy Cat Press, cozycatpress@aol.com or visit our website at: www.cozycatpress.com

COZY CAT
P R E S S

ISBN: 978-1-946063-88-5
Printed in the United States of America

10 9 8 7 6 5 4 3 2 1

Acknowledgements

This has been a busy year as far as writing goes, which keeps my editor on her toes! Thanks to Tomi Edmiston and her red-hot pen, endless work and amazing ability, my books become the best that they can be. Thank you, Tomi!

Huge thanks to my husband, Arthur Oroz, who read the manuscript and gave me his honest opinions and helpful ideas. Thank you, my dear!

Thank you to Cindy Laurin for the cover photograph.

Special thanks to my Cozy Cat publisher, Patricia Rockwell, and her team.

Many thanks to my faithful readers who expressed to me their enthusiasm and encouragement. Several of them suggested I write about Aptos, a place that is dear to my heart and therefore easy to write about.

Comments may be sent to joyceoroz@sbcglobal.net.

Chapter 1

Tolerance was never my middle name when it came to sleepover guests, but there were allowances when the guest was my wonderful Aunt Clara. At seventy-five-years old, my mother's younger sister was a bit overweight and her motor was stuck in high gear. She wasn't blessed with Mom's sense of "style" or athletic ability, but Clara was a powerhouse behind a vacuum cleaner, her muumuu swaying and white hair billowing. If only she could resist vacuuming my house before seven a.m.

Aunt Clara's new husband, Ben, had dropped her off at my house in Aromas, California, Saturday night on his way to the San Jose Airport where he took the red-eye to Ohio. He needed to go to a memorial service for his older brother and take care of family matters while there, because he had suddenly become the oldest sibling. Ben thought that my little house on five acres in Aromas would be a safer, gentler place for Clara while he was away. Safer than their home in Boulder Creek, since the forest surrounding their house was still pretty much like God made it—full of wild animals.

Besides, Clara and I were overdue for a good visit.

Aunt Clara arrived at my house an hour before May Day with one suitcase and Sara, her sweet Rottweiler. My Basset came up to Sara's knees, but Sara and Solow loved each other unconditionally, even at eleven o'clock Saturday night.

Sunday morning Sara made quite a fuss when a certain white cat named Fluffy perched herself on my front porch railing. Fluffy belonged to David Galaz, my next-door neighbor and fiancé. The big white cat was the most purr-fect kitty to everyone except my poor dog. Solow had been led on many a wild chase only to crawl home with his tail between his legs as Fluffy watched from afar, reminiscent of Lucy, Charlie Brown and the football.

Aunt Clara and I took the dogs for a walk over to David's house. Even though we shared the same property line, it was impossible to see from one house to the other because of the hilly terrain, oak trees and wild lilac bushes. We tromped through spring grass up to our knees, from my very basic backyard patio to David's lovely backyard pond, waterfall, gazebo and rose garden. I sometimes wondered why a man with so much talent, energy and good looks was engaged to me. I pinched myself for the thousandth time.

"David, look who's here," I said.

Crouched and concentrating, he finally heard us coming, raised his head and straightened his back. On the ground beside him was a green bucket full of shiny metal traps.

"Well, well, ouch." David grabbed one of his knees, then let go. "Good to see you, Clara, you too, Josie," he winked. "I'd hug you two, but as you can see, I'm filthy." He went from a squat, up to his six-foot-two height and brushed dirt off his Levis.

"Yes, my dear, you look like a handsome rooster after a dust bath," Clara laughed. "What are you doing with all these holes everywhere?"

David scrunched his face into a melodramatic scowl.

"Gophers!"

"Oh dear!"

"Don't tell me they took...." I gasped, when I spotted an empty space in the rose garden and shook my head of wavy shoulder-length auburn hair.

David nodded. "Yep, they got the big yellow rose bush, the one you loved so much."

Clara scratched her chin. "I see you have traps."

"Yeah, what do you recommend for bait?"

"A dollop of peanut butter works well. I give them the cheap brand with all the sugar in it—to rot their teeth. And if that doesn't work, I pop 'em with Ben's twenty-two. It's good target practice." Clara circled a fresh hole, studying it. "You're gonna need a lot of traps to get all these gophers."

"I have a guy who usually takes care of it for me," David lamented. "I've been calling Eddie for almost a week. No one answers. I'm just afraid these gophers will get into the apricot orchard." David wiped his brow leaving a swipe of dirt across his forehead.

"Can they take down a fruit tree?" I wondered out loud.

"Yep, they can actually kill a young tree, like the ones I planted over there." David pointed to the east side of his orchard about a hundred feet away. He had been growing apricot trees and a few pear trees for the last ten years—as long as I had known him. Recently he retired from IBM and celebrated his fifty-second birthday by planting a row of ten baby apple trees.

Clara shook her head sadly. "Unfortunately, those little monsters love young tree roots. Have you tried Juicy Fruit gum?"

"Actually, I have." David picked up his shovel. "I think they chew it until the flavor's gone and then spit it out."

"Aren't they supposed to swallow it and choke?" I said.

"Something like that," David laughed, as he poked his shovel in the sandy turf looking for suspicious gopher tunnels.

"I have an idea," Clara said, "build an owl house and let the owls take care of the problem. I'm sure you can find building instructions on the internet."

"Thanks, Clara. Sounds like a good idea…excuse me." David's phone jingled in his shirt pocket. He brought it to his ear. "Yeah, this is David…hey, Jimmy, old boy…no…mm…mmm…on his rifle? That's too bad." He winced. "Thanks for calling, and let me know if there's anything I can do." He put the phone back in his pocket.

"Bad news?" I asked.

"Yeah, they found Jimmy's brother, Eddie. It seems he drowned in the creek that runs through his place…" David stared at his dusty boots. "Jim and I have been friends since high school basketball," his voice went down to a whisper.

"That's too bad…wait a minute," I said, "I remember you telling me about Eddie's creek. You said it was only a foot deep and came from a year-round spring."

David shrugged. "All I know is what Jim just told me. He said a neighbor found Eddie face down in the water last Saturday, on top of his rifle."

"That's so sad," I said. "I don't remember ever meeting Jim."

"Big guy, buzz-cut like Eddie, but without the bushy beard…."

"No, I don't remember seeing anyone like that. I didn't even know Eddie had a brother," I said, imagining Jim as a tall quiet-type like Eddie.

David explained that he and Jim had attended the same high school, graduated from different colleges, but years later both men ended up working in the same IBM facility in San Jose. David had retired when he turned fifty-two, but Jim still worked there. Jim and Eddie had had a falling-out several years ago.

David put one knee to the ground and shoved a baited steel trap into one of a thousand gopher holes. Either he was an optimist or he was looking at the ground so we wouldn't see the tears in his eyes.

Actually, I always thought of David as the optimistic type with loads of patience, except when it came to my fascination with murder mysteries. I not only loved to read them—I loved to solve them. My mind was already focused on Eddie's murder. My body tingled as if I were plugged into an electrical charge. I didn't know Jim, but I felt sad that he had lost his estranged brother.

It looked to me like David loved being retired, except for the gopher problem. His go-to guy for odd jobs around the property had been Eddie, and now he was gone. I didn't need a handyman because my small adobe house was surrounded by weeds and oak trees. I used the "natural" low maintenance approach, especially since I needed to spend most of my time and energy working for a living. I owned my own mural painting business, Wildbrush Murals, and had two wonderful painters working for me. Alicia and Kyle knew their way around mural painting, and I was lucky to have them. Alicia was my best friend, ten years my junior and lived ten miles away in Watsonville. Kyle, also an excellent painter, was a rather shy, redheaded freshman at UCSC in Santa Cruz.

David and I had been friends for almost ten years, but recently we had become more than friends. Mom and Dad couldn't wait for us to marry, but I tended to drag my feet when it came to picking a wedding date. Not because of the trauma of losing my first husband seventeen years ago due to an eighteen-wheeler accident, but because at fifty-years-old, I loved my freedom as much as I loved David, freedom to investigate mysterious happenings—even murder.

Clara nudged me with her elbow.

"Huh? Oh…David, would you like to come over for dinner tonight?"

He looked up from the gopher hole. "Are you asking this filthy old guy to dinner?" He grinned his magical white-tooth grin. His mischievous chocolate brown eyes crinkled for a moment, but I sensed the sadness over Eddie's death that he had stuffed away for later. He picked up his bucket of traps and walked to the next hole.

"Yes, Josephine and I are inviting you to dinner," Clara jumped in.

David knelt down on one knee, loaded another trap and worked it into the gopher hole. I don't think he even noticed that we were rounding up the dogs and leaving. If concentration could kill, those nasty gophers would already be dead. Or maybe he was thinking about his deceased friend, face down in the creek.

Suddenly I wanted to drive twenty miles north to Eddie's place in Aptos (Ap-toss) to check out the creek. The little unincorporated town stretched out in all directions, rimming the Pacific Ocean to the west and stretching over the hills to a lush redwood forest to the east. The freeway separated the west side from the east side, creating six little villages within the town of Aptos.

Each little enclave, Aptos Hills, Larken Valley, Cabrillo, Seacliff, Rio Del Mar and Seascape, had its own distinct personality, topography and history. My next mural job was scheduled to take place in a 1920's mansion in Seascape, overlooking the ocean. The magnificent home was being renovated, and I would be helping with the details, such as replicating designs from the twenties in the form of large murals.

My mind suddenly switched to the eastern side of the freeway and the forested hills of Rio Del Mar. David had talked about Eddie's place—twenty secluded acres—and I could hardly wait to see it. At today's prices, the land alone had to be worth millions.

Aptos was founded in 1833, developed from a 6,656-acre land grant from Mexico. In modern times, the 1850's wharf, general store and lumber mill were all but forgotten. Sandwiched between Soquel (So-kell) and Watsonville, some twenty-four thousand Aptos residents enjoyed living in the middle of incredible natural beauty.

Sunday afternoon I tried very hard not to dash off to Eddie's creek property, but Clara was no help with that. She had a curious mind twenty years before I was even born. She always loved a good adventure.

Back at my house Sara and Solow immediately passed out on my living room floor, each claiming a small section of the oval braided rug my late grandmother had given me. But they looked up as Clara and I tiptoed to the front door, feeling a bit guilty for not inviting them. But how could we? I owned one vehicle, an older red Mazda pickup with two front seats only. Sure, I could have borrowed David's Jeep and listened to all the reasons I shouldn't butt into Jimmy's affairs. In my experience, it was easier to explain things after they were already done, especially if things worked out well.

Sunny skies and pure clean air beckoned as we left my beloved Aromas behind us. Clara and I sang along with Elvis and his beautiful version of "How Great Thou Art," as my faithful truck roared past miles of lettuce and berry fields. We crossed Watsonville and took Highway One north about seven miles to the second Aptos exit, "Rio Del Mar."

"Are you sure you know how to get there?" Clara asked as she pulled a Santa Cruz County map from the glove compartment.

"I know how to get this far. The rest is up to my navigator."

"Your navigator needs a nap, but I'll try." Clara dug through her frayed, multi-colored quilted hippy purse that clashed beautifully with her pineapple-patterned muumuu. She finally found her cheaters, placed them on her nose and wrestled the map open.

By that time I really needed to know which way to turn, so I pulled the truck to a stop at the side of the road.

"What's the name of the road we're looking for?" Clara asked.

"David mentioned that Eddie lived on Trickle Creek Road, and he said something about Trout Gulch."

"I see it, Josephine. Just drive two inches, I mean a couple of miles north on Freedom Boulevard and then make a right on Trout Gulch." She folded the map and watched the scenery go by. In no time, we were dealing with stop signs and a very old railroad trestle. We moved slowly through the little Aptos village and eventually turned right at the stoplight onto Trout Gulch, a two-lane curvy road heading east into the mountains.

After about five miles, I sighted a sad little sign—old, faded and hanging by one rusty nail. When I tilted my head, it read, "Trickle Creek." Under that sign was a similar hand-painted sign that read, "No trespassing." We turned left onto the unpaved, narrow, rutty road, and then took a gentle left onto Eddie's driveway.

"Isn't it lovely here in the forest?" Clara swooned. "It's still damp from winter, and—look—someone got stuck in the mud." The tracks were deep and we rolled right into them.

"I just hope we don't break an axle," I grumped, imagining two helpless women lost in the woods being chased by cougars through sucky mud. The scenario ran through my head several times, like a roadrunner cartoon.

"Careful," Clara groaned as she grabbed my arm.

"Don't worry, Auntie, I'm looking straight ahead. I'm ignoring the ravine." Actually, the deep hollow on our left was why my truck hugged the bank on our right. Laurel branches slapped and scraped Clara's window. She sat, eyes wide, leaning toward the windshield, muttering driving suggestions. As we careened down the steep grade, she pushed her foot to the floor as if there were a second brake on her side. I was already worried about the return trip when we made the last turn and came to a stop on flat land.

The driveway had come to an end—not a structured end, it just fizzled out. Someone else had come to the end before we arrived.

"Hey, Josephine, a sheriff's car," Clara said. "That sheriff looks familiar, but I don't remember the bald spot. Do I know him from somewhere?"

"That's our friend, Calvin Sayer. I don't see anyone with him." *Thank goodness*, I thought to myself. Sayer's partner could be a real pain in the posterior. Denise Lund was the complete opposite of Calvin. She was tall and skinny with straight blond hair pulled into a tight bun. Her pale white skin and cold blue eyes could give a person frostbite. He, on the other hand, had brown skin, dark eyes, frizzy black-going-gray hair, a warm smile and an occasional sense of humor.

Clara and I climbed out of the truck at the same time Sheriff Sayer pulled himself out of his vehicle. His eyes looked sleepy like he'd been napping.

"Ladies, here to view the meadow?"

"It's a real stunner," Clara said, "but we're here because of a murder."

"That figures," he said, his full lips trying not to smile. "Can I help you with something?"

"Actually, you can. Where is the creek?" I asked.

"Which part of the creek?"

"The part where they found Eddie…."

Sayer's eyes widened as he put on an exaggerated look of surprise. "Oh, that part. I guess you missed the yellow tape at the top of the driveway, you know, where you can turn right or keep going down here to the meadow. I'm just wondering how we're going to get back to the top." He looked at his mud-caked tires, scratched his head, and looked at my muddied truck.

While the sheriff and I discussed the return trip, Clara found a nice log to sit on where she could soak up some sun and watch a family of deer on the opposite side of the meadow. The discussion ended and I sat down beside my aunt, while Calvin did a couple of stretching exercises to get the kinks out of his legs. He asked if we were ready to leave since my truck was blocking his departure.

Clara looked up. "I could spend all day here...I mean, Josephine, are we ready to go?"

"Sure," I said, as I pulled on Clara's arm until she was fully upright. It seemed a shame to leave such a lovely spot, but there was a mystery to be solved.

Half-an-hour later, after an intense and grueling mud-spattering ride up Eddie's driveway, the sheriff, Clara and I clambered out of our vehicles. We were parked on flat ground under a canopy of oak branches with Eddie's old green pickup truck and a blue Harley Davidson motorcycle on our left and a six-foot-high woodpile on our right. The air was warm, clean and lightly scented with bay leaves. Puddles of sunlight brightened the mulchy ground.

Two blue jays warned each other of our arrival.

The three of us stood a few feet in front of the vehicles, next to a crystal clear miniature creek approximately three-feet wide at its widest point. My fingers touched the pebbly bottom without my elbow getting wet. It was all so lovely until I thought about Eddie falling on top of his rifle into the water. Why did he need a rifle? Was someone threatening him?

Calvin and Clara leaped across the creek and wandered to the end of the driveway. I followed the crystal stream of water as it narrowed and tumbled down the bank toward the screened opening of a pipe leading to a very large green holding tank tucked into the steep wooded hillside below. Heading down the mountain to my right was a series of rickety wooden stairs and walkways zigzagging about fifty feet down to a cabin-style house. Only the chimney and part of the roof were visible from where I stood in the parking area.

"Auntie, are you sure you want to go down there?" I said as her seventy-five-year-old body began the steep trek down to the cabin. "What goes down must come up," I warned.

Sheriff Sayer caught up to my aunt and patiently held onto her elbow as they traversed the maze of wooden walkways and three sets of stairs. I followed them, thumping down the last set of five stairs and across the creaky redwood deck to the front door. Calvin knocked. We didn't expect anyone to come to the door—it was just customary to knock. I peeked in the living room window, putting to memory a brown leather couch with a light blue lap blanket draped over the back and an orange open-weave shawl or lap blanket next to the blue one. Poor Eddie must have had a circulation problem or else his furnace was on the blink.

When I looked up, Clara had disappeared from view.

Sheriff Sayer thumbed me that she had gone around the corner.

I walked across the three-sided wrap-around deck and found my Auntie standing at the end of the railing looking down.

"What's so interesting down there...?" I felt a bit dizzy, as my gaze traveled down the steep ferny hillside.

"See those ferns?" she whispered. "I saw something crawling through the ferns, under them actually."

"What do you mean by something? Like a deer or a skunk?"

"I don't know if it was an animal or...."

"What else could it be but an animal crawling around in that dense greenery? Sure is quiet out here since the blue jays quit snarking at each other."

Clara shivered.

We turned and headed back to Calvin who was busy snapping pictures of the front door and the welcome mat. He pulled on plastic gloves and began carefully collecting tiny pieces of this and that, and dropped them into a small plastic bag.

"Sheriff Sayer, where's your partner?" I asked, trying to sound concerned.

He looked up. "She's on leave."

"What does that mean?"

"Actually, she kinda had a melt-down."

In my mind I pictured an iceberg named Denise Lund melting into a puddle of blue water.

"What exactly is a melt-down?" Clara demanded.

"Woman stuff, I think," Sayer said. "She hasn't come to work in over a month."

"A whole month?" Clara exclaimed.

"Maybe you'd like to visit her…see how she's doing?"

"Don't tell me—you haven't gone to see her…?" My aunt cocked her head, as her eyes drilled into the poor man's forehead.

"Actually, I think she needs a woman to talk to." He shook his head, looking like the average puzzled male when it comes to women's issues.

"Okay, Sheriff, where does she live?" Clara asked.

I closed my eyes and hung my head. The last thing I wanted to do was talk to the melted Ice Queen. But minutes later my aunt had Denise's address and promised Sayer that we would drop by and check on her.

Chapter 2

Where did the time go? I thought to myself. Aunt
Clara and I had been so absorbed in Eddie's crime
scene and unusual digs that we forgot we had invited
David over for Sunday dinner. Suddenly, I noticed the
sun had disappeared and the parts of sky that were
visible through small spaces between the oak branches
had turned orange and red. Lucky for me, we didn't
have time to drop in on Denise—we didn't even have
time to cook a proper meal.

Clara thought we should stop at the barbecue place
in Watsonville and order ribs with coleslaw and cheese
buns. I would never say no to a plan like that.

The remains of a fiery sunset flashed in the rear
view mirror as we sped along San Juan Road toward
Aromas. My little truck rocked with old music and the
lip smacking smell of ribs and barbecue sauce.

"Josephine, who's following us?"

"What do you mean?" I glanced in the rearview.

"Whoever it is has one yellowish headlight and one
bluish light," she said.

"What makes you think he's following us?"

"I'm very observant...."

"Except when you're not," I laughed.

"Seriously, Josephine, I noticed the pickup way
back when we were leaving Eddie's place. It had those
mismatched headlights. Sheriff Sayer pulled out first,
we followed him down Trout Gulch, and the truck was
behind us the whole way, until we turned onto East
Lake and ordered takeout."

"I remember seeing an old green pickup parked next to a beautiful blue Harley at the end of Eddie's driveway," I admitted, "but no one was around to drive it."

"Maybe Eddie's ghost is driving."

I cocked my head to one side, "I can't believe you said that."

Aunt Clara laughed, "I don't know who's driving, but he must have been on Eddie's property. Maybe he's a shy mountain man looking for a good woman."

"Maybe you're right, but why is he following us?"

Clara laughed until she was out of breath and gulping air. "Maybe he's going to Aromas to see you, Josephine."

"Must be a coincidence," I muttered. But I never believed in coincidences and neither did my aunt. Besides, I remembered seeing an old green pickup full of rust spots parked in front of the ACE hardware store next to Banjo BBQ. Way too much coincidence!

"What are you doing, Josephine? This is no place to pull over...."

"I'm proving a coincidence," I said, as my truck idled at the side of the road. An old green pickup lumbered by and kept going until his one taillight disappeared around a bend in the far distance. We pulled back onto the road and proceeded on our way to Aromas.

I had forgotten all about the truck until we drove into my neighborhood and looked up David's driveway. There it was. We watched a tall lanky dark-haired man, wearing bib overalls, climb out of the front seat and walk over to David.

I parked behind the old green pickup.

David and his friend were doing a little back slapping in the driveway, as we walked up to them.

"Jimmy, I'd like you to meet my fiancée, Josephine Stuart, and her Aunt Clara." David wrapped an arm around my waist, leaned down and kissed my forehead.

"Glad to meet you, Jimmy," Clara said. "Are you boys hungry?"

"I didn't mean to interrupt anything...." Jimmy said, apologetically, eyes trained on his thumbnail.

"Don't worry, old buddy, I'll bet a hundred dollars there's a whole bunch of barbecued ribs in Josie's truck. I can smell them from here," David laughed. "Let's all go inside, I'm starving. I've been working in the orchard all day."

"That's the reason I'm here, David," Jimmy said, as the guys carried two big bags of take-out into the house. "I'm working through Eddie's calendar, trying to help his customers...."

"Don't worry about me, Jimmy, I'm working on the gopher problem myself."

"Catch anything?" Jimmy set one bag of food on the kitchen counter.

Clara and I set more bags of food on the counter.

"Not yet," David groaned dramatically. "I should have paid attention to Eddie's technique. He sure was good at catching gophers, bless his heart."

"He was good at a lot of things," Jimmy mumbled. "I just can't understand how he could be dead. My brother could handle almost anything; he had great instincts. I could never do the things he did."

"Yeah, but you're a married techie with a kid in college. Eddie wouldn't know how to function in your world." David set his bag of take-out on the counter and began pulling out containers of hot saucy meat, while I emptied the salad and bun bags.

"True," Jimmy said, holding the last container in mid-air. "Did you invite five more people to dinner?"

"No, they gave us a lot of food…oh, I'll be back," I said. "I need to feed Solow and Sara and bring them over here."

"I've heard a lot about that dog of yours." Jimmy let out a nerdy laugh, as he walked my auntie and me to the door.

"All good, I'm sure. I'll help Josephine with the dogs," Clara said, as we left the guys and walked down David's blacktop driveway, armed with flashlights. We turned left on Otis Road. The red sunset had turned purple, almost black. A big bright silver moon was rising behind us, throwing spooky shadows in front of us as we walked. A hundred yards up the road we turned left onto my long gravel driveway. It was a longer but easier walk than venturing through the back acres.

Solow and Sara jumped and twirled, so happy to see us, not to mention hungry for their raw meat and kibble dinners.

We sat at the kitchen table for a couple minutes while the dogs horsed down their food.

"I wonder what Jimmy's wife is like," Clara said, as we grabbed our jackets from the hall closet and steered the dogs out the front door.

"All I know is that they have one kid, but I don't remember if it's a girl or boy," I said.

"Look at this, Josephine, someone sent you a package."

I pointed my flashlight at a package wrapped in brown paper with the wrong house number on it. "This is for David." I tucked the package under my arm and held Solow's leash with the other hand. Crunching down the driveway, Clara and I admired the bright moon to our right and twinkling stars off to our left.

"Do you think it's medicine, tools or a new pair of hiking boots?" Clara said, as she eyed the package I was carrying.

"I don't know what's in the package, but I know that I'm hungry and—look—the guys are standing on the porch waiting for us." They ushered us into the dining room where David had placed dishes, napkins and silverware around the table. In the middle were two candles poking out the tops of two empty wine bottles. Hot wax ran down the sides of the bottles, reminding me of a stormy night ten years ago when David and I drank a toast to our new friendship in light cast from those same candles.

A whole decade had passed since the dark stormy night when I met David for the first time. I had been driving down Otis, heading to Aromas to buy candles, when I came upon a large tree limb and a tangled power line resting ominously on top of a Jeep. I parked at the side of the road and quickly grabbed my flashlight and umbrella from the glove box. The rain pounded and the wind roared, as the elements conspired to rip my umbrella to shreds. A stand of giant eucalyptus trees had been under assault for several hours, their limbs strewn all over the road.

Water swirled around my tennis shoes as I crept toward the pinned vehicle.

"Don't come any closer!" a husky voice shouted. "There's a live wire!"

"What do you want me to do?" I shouted over the roar of the wind.

"Call 911 on your cell phone. I can't reach mine."

"Okay!" I shouted and ran back to the truck. I climbed into my seat and pulled the phone out of my purse with shaky wet hands. There must have been a million emergencies going on. The operator put me on hold. My heart pounded in my chest as I watched the sparking wire curl this way and that while the eucalyptus swayed dangerously overhead. Once the call was placed, my heart slowed down from double-time to time-and-a-half.

I still remember waiting what seemed like hours for the fire truck, followed by a truck from the electric company to arrive. It probably took ten minutes in real time. I watched as the utility guy removed the wire, and the firemen pulled a man out of the Jeep and onto a gurney. By that time, an ambulance had arrived—just in time to haul him off to the hospital.

Should I go to the hospital? No, I didn't even know him. I was happy he was safe and left it at that. But that wasn't the end of it.

The next morning there was a knock on my front door. Wearing a baggy t-shirt and sweat pants and my hair springing out in all directions, I opened the door. Blinking into the morning sun, I glimpsed a tall handsome man wearing a leather jacket, Levis and black boots. He had a quirky smile, white teeth and dark dancing eyes.

"Hi neighbor," he said. "I'm David Galaz."

"Hi, I'm Josephine," I stuttered, gazing into those amazing eyes.

"I wanted to thank you for saving my life last night."

I liked the sound of his voice.

"Can I repay you with breakfast at the grange?"

We shook hands. "That's right, this is Sunday when the grange puts on a pancake breakfast. I've heard that it's really good," I said, and then I remembered how disassembled I must have looked in my comfy old sweats. I pushed a clump of hair away from my left eye. Ten years later, I still remembered my first impression, that the man looked strong but tender…actually, he had me on the first smile.

"You don't have to dress up or anything," he offered, glancing at the ceiling.

"Can you come back in half an hour, when I'm freshened up a bit?"

"Ah, sure, pick you up in half an hour," he said, slowly backing through the doorway and across the front porch. He turned his body to leave, but teetered on the top step and caught himself just in time. To my delight, he looked back and grinned—eyes twinkling.

"I can drive…." I said.

"That's okay, the Jeep's in the shop but I have another car."

We spent the whole day together, starting with breakfast at the grange and ending with spaghetti and an old movie on TV, as two candles burned down to half their original size.

"Josephine, are you going to sit down?" Clara asked.

Pulling my thoughts back to the present, I sat down in the chair next to David. "I see you put out extra napkins. Good thinking."

"If he was really smart, he'd have given each of us a bib," Clara laughed. Unfortunately, my aunt and I had a history of food landing on our well-developed chests. But Clara's sister—my mother, never had to wash barbecue sauce or mustard off her blouses. Everything about Leola was neat and clean.

"Jimmy, please pass the salad," I said.

He handed the salad to me and went back to his maniacal attack on a rack of gooey ribs. The ribs were good, but Jimmy made them look like the best thing he had ever sunk his teeth into.

"Have some more meat, Jimmy," Clara said, holding the platter out to him.

He stuck his fork into the red goo and plopped another section of ribs on his plate. David went to the kitchen for more napkins. Meanwhile, Sara and Solow repositioned themselves behind Jimmy's chair, since he was the last to finish his meal. Jimmy cleaned his chin and wiped a smudge of barbecue sauce off his overalls with the new stack of napkins.

"There's one more rib here," Clara pointed out to Jimmy.

He shook his head and stifled a burp as his cheeks reddened. "I think I ate too much already."

David poured coffee and returned to his seat. "Jimmy's a vegetarian."

"Coulda fooled me," Clara laughed.

Jimmy pressed his lips together, looking like he might lose his dinner.

David laughed. "Fiona's a real vegetarian…and Jimmy is too when they're together."

"I tend to overdo it when I'm on my own," Jimmy confessed. One more muted burp, an "excuse me," and he began to relax a bit. "My wife is strongly against the murdering of animals."

"Never mind that people have been eating meat since the beginning of time," Aunt Clara commented.

Jimmy rolled his eyes up to the ceiling. "She recently held a demonstration at the San Diego Zoo demanding they eliminate all cages. Lucky for everyone, the demonstrators were escorted out of the park."

"How can there be a zoo with no cages?" Clara asked.

"Exactly the point," Jimmy laughed.

"Some studies show that plants have feelings…." I said.

"Well, if we can't eat meat and we can't eat plants, the next generation will have to be robots," David concluded. "Which reminds me, did anyone else see the little helicopter drone yesterday?" He looked directly at me.

"No, I wasn't home most of the day…."

"It went up Otis and disappeared, came back over my property, hovered and then took off toward town. I think it was taking pictures."

"Or some neighbor kid built himself a drone and was having fun," Clara chuckled.

"The package Josie got by mistake…it's a drone, at least it will be when I get it assembled," David said.

"Drones can be a big problem at the airports…." Jimmy added with a frown.

"That sounds like Fiona talking," David snickered. "I promise not to take it to the airport."

"Good!" Jimmy laughed. "You're right about Fiona, but she's right once in a while," his lips curled into a cautious little smile. "She tends to over worry about things."

We all sensed that Jimmy's words were an understatement. He seemed to be a quiet, shy guy who lived his life under his wife's thumb. I thought about my mom and dad's marriage. They were very devoted to each other, as they enjoyed their separate ideas, hobbies and friends. But they often enjoyed their mutual friends and activities as well.

"So, Jimmy, when was the last time you talked to Eddie?" I said. David gave me a "warning" kind of look, but I ignored it. "Who do you think might have been on his property? Did he have any enemies, like a cranky neighbor or someone who didn't like his work?"

Jimmy looked down at his hands like a third-grader not wanting to read aloud in front of his classmates. "It seems my brother was renting out part of his house. Last winter I needed to borrow a skill saw." Jimmy forced a laugh. "Fiona had an idea for a Christmas decoration, and I'm not exactly a tool guy. Anyway, I followed Eddie down to the basement and there were all these new tools, cans of paint, wood, you name it. It looked like a hardware store. He was so happy to be getting paid for storing the stuff."

"Why would he do that?" I said.

"Did he need the rent money?" Clara asked.

"I don't think so. I think my brother was always insecure when it came to money. It started a long time ago when Eddie and I were teens living on our own."

"Teens…on your own?" Clara looked horrified.

"We grew up in Weedpatch, outside of Bakersfield. When we were twelve and fourteen, our little sister had surgery for cancer, and she didn't pull through…." Jimmy looked away. "Dad took off for Alaska to work on an oil rig, and Mom just sat in her rocker day-after-day. Eddie and I had to fend for ourselves and try to keep food on the table for Mom, even though she ate very little. That went on for about a year; then Dad's checks quit coming, and Mom lost her mind. We put her in a home with about a dozen other mentally ill folks, and hitched our way north to the bay area." Jim stared at his hands.

"Eddie was fifteen and able to grow a few hairs on his chin, trying to look older. He worked hard so I could finish high school. He was always fixing machinery, building things, painting houses and doing yard work. It just came naturally to him. He worked hard and saved his money. By the time I was old enough to join the Navy, he had already bought property in the Aptos hills. The Navy gave me an education in electronics."

"So you think Eddie rented out the basement because he thought he needed money?" I asked.

"I think it was because we were dirt poor for several years. Maybe our struggle had a long-term effect on him."

David's house had become very quiet, like when everyone holds their breath. Even the dogs were listening and waiting to hear the end of the story.

Chapter 3

Monday morning began like most mornings, sun rising, birds chirping and a vacuum cleaner roaring through the house with Aunt Clara behind it. She needed to feel needed, and I needed to get on the road to my new mural job in the Seascape area of Aptos. My heart thumped with excitement whenever I thought about the stately mansion overlooking beautiful Monterey Bay. The rooms to be painted had already been measured, sketched and the ideas and drawings approved by Mrs. Staley, with a nod from Mr. Staley as he puffed smoke from his pipe.

My little red Mazda truck was loaded to the gills with paint, tarps, ladders and such. A Snug Top kept everything covered and secure while I drove north as far as the Larkin Valley Road exit, cruised down the off-ramp and tugged the steering wheel into a hard right turn, following the loopty-loop until I was headed west. A couple more turns and suddenly a view of the Pacific Ocean filled the horizon, sparkling in the morning sun. Too bad Clara didn't come along, she would have loved the view, but Clara had promised David she would help him catch those nasty gophers.

Mindless driving was a skill I had cultivated over the years. It came in handy that morning, allowing me to indulge in thoughts of dinner at David's the night before. Jimmy could eat barbecued ribs as well as anyone but had paled when hard physical work was mentioned. Even though he was six-foot-one and weighed almost two hundred pounds, he wasn't able to do most of the things his smaller brother Eddie had done, and David told him so. There didn't seem to be any hurt feelings between them, just relief on Jimmy's part that he didn't have to do the dirty work of catching gophers, mending fences and digging ditches. To Jimmy, something like fixing pipes under the house was an unthinkably dirty job. Just the mention of spiders had him sounding like he was more than ready to go back to his projects at IBM.

Clara asked what the projects were.

Jimmy's eyes brightened. "I'm sorry. Clara, but I can't talk about it."

My aunt nodded her head knowingly, as if she had one foot in her old-fashioned world and one foot in the competitive world of technological secrets. In reality, she didn't even own a smart phone. I wasn't much better, but at least I had a driver's license and an old cell phone. For me, being an artist by trade was the perfect excuse for not boning up on apps and such.

Still thinking about the night before, I arrived at the Staley Mansion, slipped out of my truck and walked across a wide, cobbled parking area where two carpenters and an electrician had parked their pickups. They all had mega tool boxes in their truck beds, but a certain white Ford 150 with the giant built-in tool box looked familiar. I laughed when I saw a young man with a slight limp and a blond ponytail coming toward me. His blue eyes twinkled and his smile was contagious.

"Hey, Jo, Mrs. Staley said you were coming," he grinned, lifting my heaviest canvas bag from my grip.

"Thanks, it's great to see you, Chester. What projects are you working on here?"

"Little of this, little of that—new wainscoting in three of the bathrooms and the utility room. Today we start replacing the ceiling panels in the library...."

"Oh, I wish you weren't. The original panels are beautiful...."

"Wait till you see the replacement—all copper—arts and crafts period. The panels came from an old bank in San Francisco." Chester looked up two stories at the shingled roof. "My guys are installing skylights and new flashing on the chimneys."

"You have guys?"

His smile broadened. "'Mathus Maintenance': what do you think?"

"I think your business will be a great success," I said, as we strolled across the driveway. Without warning, Chester and I brushed shoulders with a bald man, mid-fifties, carrying lots of height, weight and attitude as he rushed across the parking area toward his truck.

"What's his problem?" I asked.

"Some of my work used to be his work, and Rod's never happy anyway."

"So Rod's a competing contractor?"

Chester nodded.

"Why didn't the Staleys hire one contractor for everything?"

Chester looked around. "Because they're rich but cheap—always picking the lowest bid. I happened to be between jobs, so I bid low and got the house improvement projects. Mostly carpenter work," he grinned. "Rod got the yard work. He hates yard work and his guys are just as bad. They don't know a geranium from a cactus."

We walked along a wide cobbled path leading to the back yard. Chester entered the two-story hundred-year-old stucco classic through a rear door, just a plain wooden door, not the series of large French doors facing a slate patio over-looking steep cliffs and a sandy beach seventy-five feet below.

Chester held the back door open for me as waves pounded and gulls squawked. We entered a little room where an under-achieving antique light sconce on the wall rendered a bit of gloomy light, nothing compared to the brilliant sunlight we had just left. The light was so dim I almost tripped on the first of four steps leading up to a spacious laundry room.

Chester led the way upstairs. "Where are your painters?" he asked.

"Alicia will be here around noon. She has a dental appointment this morning, and Kyle has finals all week. I'm pretty sure he'll be here next week."

"Here's the laundry room," he said, pointing to a pristine utility room.

"Do you think Mrs. Staley actually does the laundry?" I laughed.

"I doubt it—that's what the help is for. They have the Thompsons—Betty and Nibs."

"What, no chauffeur? I quipped.

"Nope, the Staley's enjoy driving their matching Maseratis, but Nibs is the one who keeps the cars in perfect condition."

As we moved through the first floor of the Staley house, many of the rooms were familiar to me. I had bid on and designed murals for the dining room, living room and master bedroom. We had discussed ideas for one of the powder rooms, and Mrs. Staley said they might want me to paint something on a short concrete wall in the back yard.

Chester stopped walking and motioned for me to check out the library. I stepped into a high-ceilinged room with ten-foot-high mahogany bookcases covering every wall. He flipped on the light switch. Dozens of small crystal lights embedded in the octagonal ceiling and in the woodwork all around us twinkled. The library was unusually well lit for a retro room of its kind. My hand instinctively wanted to feel the curves in the carved wood and the contours of the cut glass on each little light.

"Hey, Jo, don't touch that!" Chester said under his breath, quickly pulling my hand away from a light fixture.

"What's the big deal...?"

He smiled and poked a small button positioned right next to the light I had just fingered. Like an old spooky movie, a four by ten-foot section of bookcase swiveled open, revealing a narrow, shadowed staircase leading downward. A very old sconce like the one I saw in the basement lit the area—barely.

I gasped.

"Shhh, that's nothing." Chester smiled, as he reached over to the other side of the little light fixture and pushed another button. A second section of bookcase opened, giving us a glimpse of a staircase heading upward. He quickly pushed the button again and the section closed neatly.

"Can I close the downstairs one?" I asked.

"Yeah, but you don't know anything about this—okay?"

"Okay," I pledged and pushed the proper button.

The bookshelf quietly closed.

Footsteps stopped at the door. Liana Staley peeked into the room.

"Josephine, lovely to see you, dear. I guess you've already met my contractor...."

"Hi Liana, Chester and I go way back."

"Construction projects," Chester quickly clarified.

She nodded at the handsome ponytailed contractor. Even though Liana was twice his age, she still had a girlish twinkle in her eyes, at least when Chester was around. Her tall, slightly plump body was held erect, chin up as if pictures were about to be taken. And every dyed red hair on her head was perfectly held by a silver hair clip at the nape of her neck.

"Last year Chester installed all these lovely crystal lights," she swooned. "Now, Josephine, come with me, and we'll get you started on the living room wall. Chester has already finished installing the new wainscot, and the upper walls have been freshly painted with semi-gloss paint, as you instructed." She whirled around and headed down the hall, her sensible heels tapping the shiny wood floor.

Chester and I followed the hollow sounding clatter, weighted down with my heavy canvas satchels full of paint gear. We entered the spacious living room, featuring a perfect view of the patio and the ocean beyond, through four lovely French doors. Liana and I gazed at the water as if we were seeing it for the first time, probably because the water was never the same exact color twice. Three weeks ago, when I measured the room, the water had been a deep blue—turning to a frothy lime green near the shore. This time it was pure sparkling silver, as the sun headed toward its zenith. We watched tiny fishing boats scurrying back to Santa Cruz with their "morning catch." Finally, I turned away from the mesmerizing bank of glass and noticed that Chester was gone.

"He'll be back with your ladder," Liana smiled.

"I'll go get my paint box and a few other things," I said, heading out of the room.

"Josephine, use the front door…please."

"Thanks," and off I went. This was not the first time in my career I had noticed unequal treatment of male workers. Employers were usually very kind to me, sometimes offering lunch—while the male construction workers typically had to use back entrances and outside porta-potties. I suspected "Charming Chester" was like me, another exception to the rule.

By noon I had chalked in the placement of basic features of the mural: the horizon line, boulders in the foreground and an island in the distance—all taken from the Staley's favorite vacation photo of a beach in Southern California. Working with a ten-foot ceiling and three feet of wainscot, we had a seven-foot by twenty-four-foot stretch of wall to paint. Ocean water would fill the bottom two feet of space, and a dramatic sky would cover the upper five feet, giving the room an expansive and airy feeling. Sadly, our backs would be to the real ocean view as we painted.

"Daydreaming?" Alicia asked as she entered the room.

"Hi, Allie, just wondering how much detail to put on the island. I think we should build the island and then figure out what to put on it later."

"Good decision," she said, setting her purse down on a chair. She then positioned her three-foot ladder in front of the wainscot. The living room furniture had been relocated across the room, leaving a ten-foot by twenty-four-foot pathway. Nothing stood in our way, except the natural nervousness that came at the beginning of every job—the first stroke of paint on an empty wall.

"Am I the cloud maker?" Allie asked, as she examined the color sketch.

"Of course, no one does them better than you."

I stirred a glop of cobalt blue into two quarts of titanium white Nova acrylic paint. When the colors were completely combined, I poured half of the light blue mixture into another container and added more blue. Half of that mixture was poured into another container and mixed with a bit more blue, creating a third and darker shade of sky-blue. While I mixed the paint, Alicia taped the wood trim framing the wall, and arranged the tarps to protect the wood flooring.

When I had finished mixing blue paint, I unscrewed switch plates from each end of the wall, quickly sanded them by hand and used a brush to coat them with white primer paint. When the primer dried, I would give them a coat of the original wall color. They would be screwed back in place and painted as part of the mural. After that, they would be clear-coated for protection.

Standing on the six-foot ladder, Alicia began rapidly painting a two-foot by twenty-four-foot swath of the darkest blue across the top of the mural area. Standing on the three-foot ladder, I followed behind her using the medium blue, quickly blending my paint with Alicia's where they came together. We worked our three-inch-wide brushes at a furious pace. By the time I finished the second blue, Alicia was already half-way across the room with the lightest blue. The finished product was a perfectly blended sky with incredible depth.

"Oh my! You work fast," Liana said, standing in the doorway holding a large gray and white cat with the bluest Paul Newman eyes I'd ever seen.

"Skies are all about speed," I explained. "If we don't work fast, the paint dries and we can't blend the different shades of blue."

The cat named Herbert purred in Liana's arms. She nodded and walked away with the impression that we were the fastest painters in town. The truth was that the rest of the mural, especially the details, would take a lot more time.

Alicia and I took a short snack break and caught up on news. We hadn't talked on the phone in a couple of days, so there was plenty to talk about. Alicia invited Clara, David and myself to her house for Friday night dinner, and then listened to my story about Eddie's murder with tons of skepticism.

"Jo, who told you about how they found Mr. Garrett—you know, with his face supposedly down in the water, lying on top of his gun?"

"Jimmy told David, and David told Aunt Clara and me. I think David took it pretty hard, and Jimmy is really hurting. David, Eddie and Jimmy had been friends since high school."

"I guess what I want to know is, who found Eddie...?" Alicia said, as she worked a few wispy clouds into the sky.

"Aunt Clara and I talked to Jimmy last night at dinner, and he said it was the neighbor across the street. Of course, you can't see the street or any houses from Eddie's place. Apparently the neighbor woman had walked down the hill and crossed the road over to his property looking for her cat."

"So how do you know that you can't see any houses from Eddie's house?"

"Aunt Clara and I took a little trip over there...."

"I knew you were already trying to solve the murder. Here we go again," she laughed.

"We were just curious, that's all."

"So did the woman find her cat?"

"I have no idea. Jimmy said the neighbor lady didn't have her phone with her so she had to go all the way home to call 911." I shrugged, "At that point there was no hurry anyway."

"Jo, did you hear that?"

"Yeah, what was it...?"

"It sounded like metal hitting metal," Alicia said, heading around the corner to the tall cut-glass entry room windows overlooking the Staley's front yard and circle drive. I joined her. "It's not too bad, Jo...."

"Not too bad? That's my truck!" We were out the front door on the count of one, and across the driveway on the count of two. My little red Mazda had a flap of red metal sticking out about six inches, like a wounded wing over the left front tire.

"Who did this?" I said, looking around for the culprit. "Who would do this and then just drive away?"

"I saw the back end of a dark blue pickup truck just before it went around the bend," Alicia said, and pointed to a turn in the driveway, just before it connected up with Seaview Drive. The rest of the neighborhood consisted of diversely styled two and three thousand square-foot homes, averaging thirty years old and worth a bundle because of their location. But the Staley house was an anomaly, a stallion among ponies.

Chester walked up to us and shook his head. "I bet Rod has red paint on his truck," he commented, as he climbed into his pickup. He quickly fired up the engine and cranked the bulky vehicle around the loop, in the direction of Seaview Drive.

"What do you think he plans to do?" Alicia asked.

"Find Rod and punch his lights out."

"Jo, you don't mean that...."

"It's an expression. Don't worry, Chester won't get hurt," I said, unable to control the worry lines marching across my forehead.

As we turned to go back to the house, Liana stepped back inside and closed the door.

Chapter 4

Lloyd Staley appeared in the living room, silhouetted against a gaseous ball of fire heading for the Pacific Ocean. Alicia and I were arranging our paints and ladders against the mural wall so that everything would be out of the way as much as possible overnight. Lloyd walked the length of the room and back again, puffing on his pipe and working his furry gray eyebrows up and down.

"Ladies, coming along nicely, isn't it?"

"Yes, coming along," I said. "We'll be back in the morning."

"Liana and I will be taking a little trip down the coast tomorrow. Chester will let you in." Lloyd turned to stare out the windows for the millionth time, not noticing our departure. In my experience, the man seldom spoke; but when he did, he always made it sound important. Maybe it was the smooth news commentator voice, or his steady gaze and confident posture. Whatever it was, he projected strength and power. Weeks ago, Liana, Lloyd and I had gone back and forth working out details regarding my sketches. Every time there was indecision, Lloyd and his wise compromises cleared the air.

Alicia drove away after wishing me good luck with Barry, my insurance guy.

I didn't worry about good old Barry being fair, but I hadn't been able to set aside my rage. It was a blatant hit-and-run, and if Rod was a decent man he would apologize and make it right. But it was hours later and neither Rod nor Chester had made it back to the mansion. Anger aimed at Rod shared space in my head with concern for Chester.

I drove slowly through the Seaview neighborhood. The homes were lined up close together on side streets that sloped gently down toward the ocean. Closer to the water was the old Staley Mansion, perched on a fat finger of land barely attached to the neighborhood landmass, probably the first home built in the area.

My first stop on the way home would be the hardware store. Aunt Clara had called me around noon to ask if I would bring home a dozen gopher traps. It seems David and Jimmy had an emergency fence to fix in Watsonville. One of Eddie's clients had to tie his bull to a tree until the fence could be mended. Clara was left alone to fight the gophers. She sounded out of breath, as she said she had discovered a tunnel just ten feet from the new little fruit trees David had recently planted. Sara discovered the gopher first, and proceeded to dig a long deep trench with her powerful paws. Since the trench was open, with half a dozen gopher tunnels exposed, Clara wanted to fill every tunnel with a trap. And then she reminded me that we were out of peanut butter.

I took the Riverside exit off Highway One and worked my way through Watsonville to my favorite grocery store. It wasn't the biggest brightest store in town, but it was clean and the folks there were always helpful—especially my young freckled cashier friend, Robert, who was an expert when it came to fresh produce. Besides that, we had a lot in common with our interest in the news— especially murder mysteries like Eddie's.

"Jo, still setting the fashion world on its butt, I see."

"Hi, Robert, I won't make fun of your big blue apron if you don't discuss my lovely paint clothes. At least I'm wearing every color of the rainbow."

"Yeah, up to your elbows and a blue smudge across your cheek," Robert laughed. "Did you see the peaches over there? First of the year."

"Thanks, but I don't need fruit. I need peanut butter."

He thumbed aisle five.

"I know where it is, I just came over here to say, hi."

"No, you found me so you could explore my big beautiful brain," Robert laughed. "I read about Edward Garrett's murder in *The Sentinel*. It sounds pretty crazy—drowning in twelve inches of water."

"I saw the water myself. It's just a natural spring coming out of the hillside. The way Eddie's brother tells it, the neighbor lady found him when she went looking for her cat."

"I read in the newspaper that forensics found oak slivers in the back of his head—like someone had hit him with a two-by-four. Maybe he fell into that little bit of water and couldn't raise his head."

"I think you might be right," I said, as Robert followed me over to aisle five.

"Don't buy that one, they load it up with sugar," he warned. "This brand is much better."

"I'm buying the cheapest peanut butter I can find. We're going to feed it to the gophers. That is, Aunt Clara, David and I. Maybe the gophers will die happy on a 'sugar-high.' Eddie used to do all that trapping stuff. Now it's up to us."

"Oh, now I see the connection with Eddie. Good luck finding his murderer," Robert said, as he walked me up to an empty checkout lane and rang up the peanut butter. Several shoppers crowded in behind me, and Robert was stuck ringing them up.

Outside the store, I spotted my truck sitting alone and wounded in the pink light of a spectacular sunset. I checked my watch. If I hurried, I might make it to the hardware store before it closed. It was exactly seven o'clock when I parked the truck and watched a young employee carry a cluster of keys to the front entrance. I leaped out of the truck and stood on the other side of the glass door trying to explain why he should let me in. The boy's eyes grew wide as my hand motions became more demonstrative. Maybe it was the paint outfit that worried him. Maybe I was just another troll looking for a warm dry place to spend the night.

The door finally opened an inch.

"Sorry, we're closed."

"Please, I only need one thing...." I pleaded.

"Just this once," he said, in a pitch that flipped from a low bass up to a squeaky high soprano.

One of the two doors opened and I entered.

"Where do you keep the gopher traps?"

"Aisle 13, at the end."

Aisle 13 only had eight traps, but eight was better than none. I piled all eight into my arms and hurried up to the checkout. The young man was waiting for me.

"Thanks so much...." I said, as he made the sale. I paid him and dropped the traps into the passenger seat. My stomach growled. The cell phone rang.

"Josephine, dear, I promised Officer Sayer that I would call you...."

"What's this about, Auntie?"

"He told me that Denise, I mean Officer Lund, had an accident at home. He tried to talk to her but she just kept crying. He's really worried."

"And you want me to go see her...."

"Well, just a little visit so she won't have another accident."

"Auntie, what kind of accident are we talking about?"

"She accidentally took some pills...I'm worried about her too. Would you mind, dear?"

"Sure, just give me her address," I said, wishing my heart were in it.

"She lives in Aptos."

"I'm not in...never mind. I can be there in fifteen minutes." It meant back tracking ten miles north, but if something happened to Denise and I hadn't bothered to check on her...I wouldn't be able to live with myself.

Clara gave me the street and apartment number over the phone. Calvin had told her to go to the Cabrillo College area of Aptos. I knew where the college was, but not Butler Street, so I called Alicia. She looked up Butler Street on her computer. Thanks to Alicia's directions, I was able to find Denise's apartment building before dark.

When I came up to her door on the first floor, I heard noises from inside. It was crying or cussing—I couldn't tell which. I knocked on the door with my bare knuckles.

"Who is it?" Denise demanded.

I imagined her holding a pistol.

"It's me, Josephine Stuart...."

A latch clicked...a chain rattled...another click and the door opened a couple of inches.

"I'm not presentable...."

"Don't worry, Officer Lund, I'm not either. Wait till you see my paint clothes."

The door opened, Denise walked back to her nest of blankets on the sofa, and I entered the room. The furnishings were not as plain and uninteresting as I had imagined they would be. Unlike their owner, the color-scheme was warm and friendly—even interesting. Like her collection of little glass bottles of all shapes and sizes, obviously very old, since the clear glass had turned purple over time. The pillows on the sofa and easy chair were deep blue and the drapes were a light turquoise.

"You're right about the outfit, it sucks," Denise scowled.

"Yeah, I get a lot of comments like that," I lied. *Nice people wouldn't say things like that,* I thought to myself. "So, how are you feeling?"

"I'm not feeling anything, thank you. Why are you here—who sent you?"

"My Aunt Clara got a call from Calvin. He's a little worried about you."

"He showed up this morning. I wish he would mind his own business." Denise pulled a blanket up to her chin and sighed—probably a hint for me to leave.

"Have you had your dinner yet?" I asked, as my hollow tummy begged for food.

"I don't remember...."

"You didn't, did you?" I moseyed into the little kitchen and explored food possibilities. TV dinner remains cluttered the sink and filled the garbage can under the sink. "Is this all you eat?" I bellowed into the living room, as I checked the ninety-percent empty fridge and opened a few drawers.

"I'm a cop, not a foodie. What's it to you?"

"I'm starving," I said, settling into the easy chair with a menu I found in a kitchen drawer. "Do you like Chinese food?"

"Who doesn't?"

"Okay, I'm going to order some for both of us. Anything you like in particular?"

Denise shook her head full of matted white-blond hair and tightened the tie on her fuzzy blue bathrobe.

Making an executive decision, I went ahead and called in an order for both of us. My tummy groaned. I couldn't even remember lunch, but at least I had some meat on my bones. Poor Denise had no fat to spare.

"The food should be ready by the time I get to Soquel." I left right away, and yes, the food was already boxed and bagged when I arrived at The Chang Gang. On the way back to the apartment, I wondered what kind of pills Denise had taken. Did she mistakenly take a wrong prescription or take too many of something? Carrying two bags full of little white boxes containing Chinese food, I used my elbow to knock on the door. Ouch! "Don't try this at home," I said out loud. A man walking his dog down the sidewalk looked up and smiled.

The latches unlatched and chains clanked. The door opened, and Denise stepped back to her nest on the couch. I walked in, arranged the various food choices in the middle of her small kitchen table and located two clean plates, forks and serving spoons.

"Okay, Denise, dinner is served."

She took her time coming to the table, while I politely waited—when all I really wanted to do was dive into every box with my fork. I pointed to the egg foo yong, she nodded and I gave her a scoop. "Beef broccoli?" She nodded and I gave her a big scoop. "Chow Mein?" She nodded; I scooped. And so it went.

Denise played with her food, twirling noodles on her fork and stabbing at the fried rice. But I did see one of her fried wontons disappear. It was a start.

My plate emptied quickly. There was too much quiet and not enough talk, so I started to babble. "Why do I eat so fast when it's something I love? You would think I grew up with a bunch of brothers and sisters and had to fight for enough food. Actually, I grew up as an only child, and my mother was constantly telling me to slow down when I ate. Denise, do you have family in the area?"

"Just my Uncle Joe, and I can't stand him. When I saw his name on the county pedophile list, I threw up."

"Just one uncle and you don't even like him—not that I blame you. Any family in California?"

"No," she said, daintily biting into a slice of water chestnut. She stared at the kitchen clock as if to say, "Josephine, your time is up. Please go home." After swallowing a couple grains of rice, she put her fork down and moved back to her nest.

The clock ticked.

I closed the little white boxes and arranged them in her fridge.

"I think I better get home and feed my dog. Sorry to eat and run." I stood up and gathered my purse and sweater.

"You better take this food with you…."

"No thanks. I expect you to eat all of it in the next day or two."

Denise rolled her eyes. "Well, thanks for dinner."

I left in a hurry, anxious to be home with my lovable, personable Aunt Clara. We always had plenty to talk and laugh about—anything to get away from Gloomy Denise and her sad state of mind.

Traffic was light, since commute time had already passed, and I made it home in record time.

Clara sat on the sofa, head back, mouth open and a dog at each elbow—also asleep.

"Some watch dogs," I said to myself, but then I noticed Sara's eyes following me. She was sweet; but first of all, she was a Rottweiler. Quietly, she got up and followed me into the kitchen, watching me read a note stuck to the fridge with a magnet. It read: *"Josie, someone broke into Eddie's house so Jimmy and I are going over there now and will probably stay there for the night. Cops think it might be homeless people from the camp a couple of miles away. See you tomorrow evening. Love, David."*

Half an hour later, I fell asleep while watching the Ten O'clock News. My dreams were of David chasing giant gopher-animals through the orchard. I wanted to help him, but my feet were frozen and looked like raspberry popsicles. Clara's bare feet were stuck to mine, so we watched through the window as David threw spears at the creatures. The giant gophers had many fingers on each hand. They used their long fingers to gather up all the little spears David had thrown and started chucking them back at him. A spear came through the window and hit my face. I felt warm blood running down my cheek.

When I opened my eyes with a start, the TV was still on. Aunt Clara was asleep on the couch, and Solow was licking my cheek. He needed a potty break, so I let the dogs out for a minute, and then we all went to bed.

My last thought was for David's safety.

Chapter 5

Tuesday morning began with sunshine and bird songs. I asked myself, "How can I hear the birds if Aunt Clara is up and about? Why is it so quiet? No vacuum? What's going on?" Something wasn't right. I pulled on a fresh paint outfit, cut-offs and a t-shirt, and ran a brush through my tangled hair.

"Aunt Clara, where are you?" I hollered down the hall.

No one answered so I put my full attention into making breakfast. Solow and Sara were also missing—so who would share my breakfast? I reread David's note about someone breaking into Eddie's as I ate my veggie omelet and sipped coffee. One could easily conclude that the killer was the same person who had broken into Eddie's house and that we just had to find the intruder to have the killer. But there were other explanations to explore, like maybe Eddie argued with someone, made someone angry? Started a fight?

I picked up the phone and dialed Sheriff Sayer's number.

"Sheriff Sayer here." He sounded like I woke him up.

"It's Josephine Stuart. I just wanted to tell you that I saw Denise, and she's on her way to being okay because I'm going to give Aunt Clara a crack at her."

"You mean she's going to be her sunny self again," he laughed.

"I wouldn't go that far. By the way, do you have a list of Eddie Garrett's disgruntled clients?"

"That's police business…."

"I know, but I might be able to help you solve this case."

"You have something…?"

"Not exactly," I mumbled,

"When you do, let me know." He hung up.

"He hung up! I can't believe it." I stomped my foot, then I heard something and turned. "Oh, Aunt Clara, when did you get back?"

"A minute ago," she said. "Solow and Sara are off chasing Fluffy. They should be ready for a nap very soon. Yesterday David asked if I would check the traps in the morning, and I was happy to oblige."

"I don't think he meant the crack of dawn."

"Early bird gets the gopher," she laughed.

"Catch any?"

"No," Clara said, "but today I'll put out the new traps you bought."

I brought the bag full of eight traps to her. She peeked inside. "These will do the trick," she smiled. More than anything else, my aunt was a complete optimist. I usually fell a mile short when I tried to follow her example.

"Auntie, I've been thinking, Denise could really benefit from being around you and your jolly optimism. Do you have plans for tomorrow?"

"As a matter of fact, I don't. Maybe I could help the poor girl."

"When is Ben getting home?" I asked.

"Not right away. It seems he's having trouble getting his sister-in-law into a rest home. She has too many health issues, poor dear." Clara opened the front door and let in the dogs. "Josephine, what happened to your truck—it looks like it's learning to fly."

I explained to her what had happened and that reminded me that I needed to call Barry, my insurance guy. We chatted for a couple of minutes, and then I told him that a stranger had clipped my sweet little truck and took off. He wanted a police report, but I didn't have one. Alicia had taken a picture of my truck, so I told him I would send him a copy. Obviously pressed for time, Barry said everything would be okay, not to worry and hung up, right after he promised to arrange for a loaner car.

After saying goodbye to my aunt, I sped north to Highway One in my little wounded warrior truck. I took the second exit into Watsonville and pulled into the Body Shop on Green Valley Road. It wasn't the first time my truck had been injured—the people working there knew me pretty well.

"Ms. Stuart, what can we do for you...?" the office girl asked, snapping her gum.

"I'm dropping off my truck for repair work."

"Do you need a loaner?" she asked, the required paperwork already in her hands.

"Yes, I need a loaner. Here's my phone number. Can you call me today when you have an estimate?"

"We'll call you, Ms. Stuart. Sign here, here and here and you can take the purple Civic hatchback." She pointed out the side window to a lowered little car painted with metallic purple paint and darkly tinted windows on all sides. Two exhaust pipes the size of Sara poked out its rear.

My jaw gaped. "Oh my G... is that all you have?"

She smiled sweetly, handed me a key and snapped her gum.

Just a block from the shop, I stopped at a red light. In the lane next to me a young man driving a hefty pickup truck mounted on mega-size wheels, gunned his engine. The only comfort I had was knowing that the driver couldn't see my red face through the heavy tint on all the windows. Even the moon-roof was tinted. The light turned green and the truck burned rubber. I hesitated until he was half a block down the street before pushing down on the gas pedal. An impatient driver honked at me from behind. I moved forward at old-lady speed, hoping a cop wouldn't stop me on a hunch.

At the Staley Mansion, plenty of whistles and catcalls announced my colorful arrival. The Honda Civic was flashier than any of my colorful paint outfits had ever been. Climbing out of the car involved a series of seldom-used muscles—the ones that squeeze a person into a ball while exiting a clown car.

"Josephine, your taste in cars is exquisite," Alicia laughed. She grabbed my elbow and helped me to straighten up. "Chester isn't here yet, so I'm not sure how we'll get inside the house."

"Let's sit on the patio until he arrives," I suggested. We walked to the back of the house and picked a couple of comfy cushioned chairs to relax in while we watched the gentle wave-action far below. Tuesday's ocean was deep green, with a thin silver streak stretching the length of the horizon. It was only nine o'clock, but a couple of little fishing boats were already heading home with their morning catch. A picture popped into my head of a big salmon on the grill.

"Jo to earth—Jo to earth."

"Sorry, Allie, I'm just so relaxed. If someone wants to hit my car today, that's okay. I don't care, as long as I'm not in it."

Alicia laughed, "You wouldn't want any harm to come to that cute little purple car."

"Everyone in Watsonville wants to race me. The scoop on the back isn't any help," I growled, "and I have to manually shift the little snot."

"What do you think happened to Chester?" Alicia asked.

"I don't know, but I didn't see Rod's truck either. Maybe they made friends and went out to breakfast."

"And my name is Marilyn Monroe," Alicia laughed.

Just then, Chester rounded the corner of the house. The morning sun shone on his blond hair and tanned face. There was a stiff fierceness about his walk. He pulled a chair up close to us and sat down in silence.

"What happened?" I asked.

Chester stared at his hands as he massaged one hand with the other.

"I got Rod to admit he hit your truck, but he sicced his dog on me and I ended up in the emergency room. The good part of all this is that I don't limp any more." A white-toothed grin spread as deep dimples appeared. "The dog bit my good leg, so now they're even."

"Oh, Chester!" I scowled, and then we were all howling with laughter.

"Could have been worse," he added. "At least Rod got fired, and lucky for me that his dog had had his rabies shot."

"Who's going to take over for Rod?" I asked, feeling relieved that the brute was gone.

Chester pointed a thumb at his chest. "I'll have to hire more guys," he laughed. "Are you girls ready to go to work?"

Without another word, we all stood up and walked to the back door. Chester unlocked it. Once we were inside and climbed the four steps to the first floor, Chester veered off to the kitchen to make himself a cup of coffee. Young, easy to look at and good-natured, he enjoyed special treatment from most of his clients. It looked to us like he already had the run of the house.

Herbert followed Chester, his elegant white tail swishing gently side to side.

Alicia and I were surprised to see a post-it note stuck to the mural wall.

Note: *"The painting is coming along nicely. See you girls tomorrow."*

"I guess they decided to stay somewhere for the night," Alicia said.

"Isn't that romantic?" I said, as I prepared my palette. "Today we paint twenty-four feet of ocean, with no one looking over our shoulders."

Alicia and I studied three magazine pictures of ocean scenes I had brought from home. They all had similar colors, but each one had slightly different waves and white caps. We would combine the different textures and attributes into one ocean, after a short discussion. If we needed more ideas, there was the real thing right outside the windows. Like the ticking of a clock, the waves crashed all day long with comforting repetition.

On our lunch break, I called Aunt Clara. She told me that David came home around ten, and they had spent the last couple of hours setting traps. One gopher was found dead in a trap. One gopher out of a thousand!

"David's right here having lunch with me. Would you like to talk to him?"

"Yes, thank you, Auntie."

"Josie, how's it going over there?"

"Like you, we're having lunch and relaxing. It's easy to feel relaxed here, by the ocean. You can't believe how beautiful it is."

"I promised your aunt I would barbecue a tri-tip tonight...."

"Oh, David, that would be great!"

"Okay, honey, see you tonight."

"Yeah, and congratulations on getting a gopher...oh, and we're all invited to dinner at Alicia's on Friday."

"Great," he chuckled, and we hung up.

The afternoon slipped by, a peaceful ocean materialized on the wall and suddenly we painters were at a good stopping place. Alicia and I cleaned our brushes and stacked our equipment neatly against the wall. Chester usually left the job around three or four o'clock, but this time he stayed until five. He folded our ladders and leaned them against the wall.

We took turns saying goodbye to Herbert.

Chester locked up the house.

The three of us caravanned up the driveway and through the neighborhood to Highway One. Chester took the North on-ramp and Alicia took the South ramp. I crossed the freeway but at the last minute decided not to enter the freeway. Instead, I headed for Eddie's place. I told myself it was a beautiful day for a drive, and the commuter traffic would subside later. Besides, the tri-tip wouldn't be ready for a couple more hours.

Driving past Eddie's place, I discovered an apple orchard, farmhouse and barn at the end of Trickle Creek Road. The property was a sunny, old-fashioned delight surrounded by a weathered waist-high split rail fence.

An older woman, heavy-set with graying hair, hoed weeds while her scruffy yellow cat watched. She looked up when I stopped the Civic next to her fence. It was a wonder she didn't grab a shotgun when she saw the metallic purple low-rider. Maybe she didn't own a shotgun. She dropped the hoe and marched quickly toward the barn. Maybe she did have a shotgun.

I scrambled out of the car, shouted "Hello" and tried to look casual like a person who happens to wear colorful paint-stained clothing.

The woman slowed and looked over her shoulder.

"Hello." I said again. "I'm looking for the Garrett property."

She turned around and put a hand to her brow, against the imminent sunset. Walking toward me with the glare in her eyes, the middle-aged woman pointed down the road with her other hand. "That way, but there's no use going there…he's dead," she shouted. The cat curled its body around her ankles causing her to stop several yards from me. "What kind of contraption are you driving?" She pulled the cat loose and moved closer to the fence, her eyes wide.

"Oh that; it's a loaner. A guy in a hurry crashed into my truck."

"It's a jungle out there," she said.

"By the way, my name is Josephine Stuart."

"I'm Bessie Hatch."

"To tell you the truth, Bessie, I wanted to meet you because I heard that you were the one who found Eddie."

She looked down at her cat. "I was lookin' for my cat, and I found Eddie instead." She started to turn away.

"Who do you think killed him?"

"I have no idea," she muttered.

"Bessie, do you know anyone who had a grudge against Eddie?"

"How would I know? I don't meddle where I'm not wanted." She picked up the cat and stalked off toward the barn.

Settling back in the loaner, I thought about the woman's last words. "I don't meddle where I'm not wanted," sounded like she got the cold shoulder from a guy she was interested in, namely, Eddie. I cranked the wheel left, circled back down the road to Eddie's property and parked next to his green pickup truck. I hadn't seen any homeless people—or people of any kind along the way. I wondered if David and Jimmy had spotted anyone.

My plan was to take a quick look around the property, and then scoot home for the barbecue. David and I were engaged to be married, and I was the lucky one because he was an excellent cook—among other things. Whatever he saw in me, it wasn't scrumptious meals. Living alone for the last seventeen years had deadened any desire in me to become a gourmet cook.

A blue jay squawked, causing my skin to prickle as I tramped down the hillside. Laughing out loud at my skittishness, I crossed the deck and peeked in the living room window. There was the brown couch and the light blue lap blanket…but no orange shawl. "Maybe David or Jimmy moved it," I thought out loud. I walked along with one hand on the railing and gazed down at the forest of ferns where Clara had seen something moving. Nothing moved.

Breaking the absolute silence, a door slammed somewhere above me. I looked up in the direction of the driveway, but trees cluttered the view. Another door slammed. I heard voices. It sounded like two men laughing and speaking another language, possibly Spanish.

Not expecting company, my feet felt like they were nailed to the deck boards. I was frozen to the spot and the voices were coming closer. Two young men wearing work clothes were coming down the stairs. They paused for a moment when they saw me, then continued clomping down the incline. As they grew nearer, I memorized their features. The tallest fellow had a fat mustache and black hair pulled back into a knot. The other guy was heavy, had a shaved head and wore a dirty t-shirt over his big belly.

Big Belly came up to me and spoke in Spanish.

I looked at him blankly. "I'm sorry, but my Spanish is very basic," I said, not able to remember a single word of Spanish at that moment.

Mr. Mustache stepped closer and spoke in English. "What are you doing here?"

"My name is Josephine and Eddie was my fiancé's friend...."

"Like I said, what are you doing here?" he repeated.

"Just looking around. What are you doing here?" I tried to sound authoritative.

"You not my Mama!" Belly snarked. "And why you dress like that?"

Mustache pushed him away. "Josephina, you should go now—we have business here."

"Are you in the construction business?"

"Josephina, it's not your business to know—now go." He pointed at the stairs, like telling a barking dog to go home.

Feeling insulted, I quickly took my leave.

From behind, I heard one of the men say, "Nice pipes." My face burned, but I didn't look back. When I reached the driveway, I finally realized they were talking about the exhaust pipes on my loaner. My heart was pounding. The stairs and walkways had proven to be an excellent cardio workout.

Manly voices drifted up to my ears, as I inspected their big white pickup truck with the most amazing rims. I couldn't find a piece of paper in my purse so I quickly jotted down the license numbers on the palm of my hand.

Chapter 6

I must have been out of my mind Tuesday night when I told Aunt Clara to be sure and get up early the next day. It was Wednesday morning, seven a.m., and she was already dressed and ready to go. I slowly climbed up out of a deep sleep, savoring my dream about David and his magical barbecue. The mechanical gem spit plenty of fire but never burned anything. It cooked every food item perfectly, even when no one was around. The plates of barbecued food multiplied as I tried to sample every dish. Clara came along and commented on the tricked out barbecue with plenty of chrome and big smoking pipes in the back.

"Josephine, I didn't want to wake you, but we're all out of dog food."

"Can't be," I groaned and rolled over. "The bag is in the cupboard next to the fridge."

"I found the sack, but it's empty."

I pulled on my robe and stumbled down the hall to the named cupboard. Telltale kibble crumbs crunched under my feet.

"Ouch!" I looked inside the cupboard and there was the empty kibble sack. "How could it be empty?"

Solow and Sara joined us. We noticed that Sara's stomach bulged as she panted happily, and Solow's tummy was unusually round. They took turns lapping water from their water bowl until it was gone.

Clara looked at me and I looked at her. We laughed and decided the dogs wouldn't need food any time soon. My aunt had already made coffee and poured me a cup. The newspaper was spread out on the kitchen table. I was fully awake when I saw Eddie's picture on the obituary page. I read the article and discovered he had belonged to a group called Seaview Singles Club.

Aunt Clara saw the picture and read the article.

"Looks like Eddie wasn't a complete recluse after all," I said, already wondering how I could approach the Seaview Singles.

"Are you thinking what I'm thinking?" she said.

"Naturally," I winked. "All we have to do is look them up." I figured Alicia wouldn't mind checking. My phone was just a phone—but hers could perform miracles.

I arrived at the mansion and started painting but didn't mention Eddie's name to Alicia at first. Casually, I brought up the Seaview Singles. Alicia rolled her eyes and acted like she was too busy to look them up.

I pretended not to notice and kept painting.

She finally gave in, dropped her brush in water and fiddled with her cell phone. "I found it, Jo." She handed me the phone.

"Thanks Allie, now you're officially on the investigating team…."

"Oh no, you don't. It's not my thing and you know it."

"What if you end up finding the killer? You'll be so proud of yourself," I said.

She shook her head. "I'm not a natural-born snoop. I'll leave it to you and your aunt to do that. By the way, what's Clara doing today?"

"I dropped her off at Denise's apartment…."

"Denise?"

"Sheriff Denise Lund, a friend of mine. She's needing a bit of TLC right now, and I thought Aunt

Clara could do the job." I checked Alicia's smart phone. "Hey, good news, the Seaview Singles meet on the first Friday of every month at 7:00 in the evening at the Aptos Grange. Do you like potlucks?"

"Sorry, Jo, I'm busy that night," Alicia laughed.

"That would be this coming Friday...."

"Guess you won't be coming to dinner Friday. Trigger's going to make a special cucumber salad. He's been making them every night since his grandma showed him how."

"Allie, that sounds wonderful...."

"To tell you the truth, I don't think I can eat one more cucumber salad," she groaned. "But I'm happy he's interested in cooking. When he turns eleven, he'll probably change his mind about working in the kitchen."

"If I know Trigger, he will always be helping out, one way or another. Here's your phone." I handed it back to Alicia.

Alicia had spent her early childhood selling chewing gum on the streets of Tijuana. She was adopted by a wonderful couple who lived in Watsonville. Alicia went to college and married a terrific guy named Ernie. Their son, Trigger, was handsome like his father and generous like his mother. I had always been very close to the boy, since I never had children of my own.

I checked my watch. "Yikes, I was supposed to pick up Aunt Clara ten minutes ago. You can work on the clouds while I'm gone," I said over my shoulder.

The little Civic hot rod loaner revved up and peeled out. My shifting had improved—still not perfect, but better. I never thought driving could be so much fun, and no one could see me through the tinted windows. I felt impervious to criticism, until a cop got the drop on me.

"Ma'am, your driver license." He leaned closer and searched the interior of the car with quick darting eyes.

I rummaged through my purse, then the wallet.

The officer looked impatient.

"Here it is," I smiled bravely.

He took the license. "Registration," he commanded.

I leaned over to the glove box, stretched my hand into the compartment and felt around for paperwork. There was a pile of it so I grabbed the whole thing and put it in my lap. My cheeks burned as I tried to hurry through the stack.

"How about this?" I asked holding up a contract I had signed allowing me to drive the loaner. He looked it over, and then searched the interior of the car with his eyes one more time.

"Did I do something wrong, officer?"

"Ah, not exactly," he mumbled and handed back the license and contract.

"Am I free to go?"

"Yes, ma'am, drive carefully." He turned and walked back to the motorcycle he had previously parked behind a bush. I was beginning to see a pattern of unfair treatment between cheerful Chester having the run of the Staley house, and me being stopped for nothing at all—just driving a car that looked like it might possibly belong to a young gang member.

Fifteen minutes later, and almost an hour late, I knocked on Denise's door. No one answered, but I heard voices inside, so I entered. Denise and Clara were curled up on the sofa crying their eyes out over the near ending of a Gregory Peck movie, *The Yearling*. Aunt Clara put a tissue to her eyes as

Denise sobbed into her lap blanket. The movie ended, and they looked my way.

"Josephine, my goodness, is it time to go already?" Clara asked.

Denise actually had color in her cheeks. I hated to break up the visit, so I suggested we all go to town and get some lunch. Clara was more than ready for lunch. Denise asked for a minute to straighten herself up—it looked like her hair hadn't been combed since the Carter administration.

The closest place to eat was a quirky little cafe across the street from the college. People who liked paté and goat cheese, quinoa and kale were in luck. Clara and I ordered brown buns made out of hemp and chia flour, spread with a thin coat of macadamia butter and dandelion jam. Denise had the kale salad…figures. But the food wasn't important; it was the camaraderie. I had never seen Denise smile until that day at lunch, when Aunt Clara had her in stitches most of the time. Eventually I had to break up the party and go back to work.

"I have an idea," Clara said with a smile, "You can pick me up at Denise's after work."

Denise exercised her thin-lipped smile and nodded her head.

"Sounds good to me," I said, as we headed back to the car. In fact, it was a good thing to have Clara busy with Denise instead of roaming the mansion with nothing to do for the rest of the day.

Denise scrunched her long body into the back seat, and Clara rode shotgun. Before starting the engine, I turned to Denise. "If you were on patrol and you saw this car make the tiniest little mistake, would you pull the driver over?"

"Am I prone to stopping and questioning gang bangers? Is that what you're asking me?"

"Yeah, because I was pulled over today for no reason. The cop even said I didn't do anything wrong."

"Josephine, there's another side to this. Some cops steer clear of this type of car. But if the officer is riding with a partner or a dog, it's not as risky."

"But what if the driver is just a seventeen-year-old trying to impress his girlfriend with a crazy car like this one?" I said.

"If it walks like a duck—it's a duck," she shrugged.

"Are you anxious to get back in uniform?"

Denise's white face paled. "Soon, I hope." She looked at the floor.

I dropped Clara and Denise at the apartment, continued a couple of miles across Aptos to the Staley Mansion and parked next to an official Santa Cruz County Sheriff's cruiser. Officer Sayer sat behind the wheel working on a crossword puzzle. He finally looked up, saw me and climbed out of the vehicle.

"This is an unexpected surprise," I said. "You'll be glad to know that my Aunt Clara has transformed your partner into an actual human being."

"No more crying…?"

"Only when watching sad romantic movies."

"Really? I mean, ah, I'm here on business." His eyes settled on my loaner as he spoke. "Ms. Quintana said you'd be right back." He reached into the front seat of the cruiser and pulled out a folder. "Where have you been in that car?"

"I had a lunch date," I smiled, "with Denise and my Aunt Clara."

Officer Sayer opened the folder. "So, I'm wondering if you've seen any of these guys."

I tried not to look shocked, but Sayer read my face immediately.

"Where did you see them?" he asked.

"I've never seen this one." I pointed to a ruddy-faced guy in his thirties wearing a knitted cap and a tattoo on his neck. "But I saw these two at Eddie's house. They were driving a big Chevy pickup with tricked out rims. Do you want the license plate number?"

"Sure." Calvin blinked his eyes, cocked his head but didn't say what was on his mind.

"You're wondering how I got this," I said, pointing to the scrap of paper I had just handed him. "It was easy; I wrote it on my hand while they were down at the house. Later I copied it onto paper." I didn't tell him how hard my heart had been beating, wondering if the two men would catch me before I had time to drive away.

"Are they suspects?"

"Police business."

Before I had time to object, Calvin climbed into his car, made a u-ey and disappeared up the driveway. Looking toward the house, I saw a couple of guys on the roof replacing the flashing around three chimneys. I wondered if the men had been able to hear our conversation from up there.

It was a good thing my mural project was a simple one. I had painted so many seascapes over the years that my mind was on "automatic," which allowed me to think, paint and chew gum all at the same time.

"Earth to Jo," Alicia quipped. "Are the clouds okay?"

"Oh yeah, actually they're perfect. They're saying, 'It's a beautiful day, but there's a chance of rain on the way.'"

Alicia said, "I think the clouds are saying, 'What a lovely day now that the rain is over.'"

Chester walked into the room. "Josephine, I need your opinion on something."

I put my brush in water, followed him down the hall, entered the stately library and looked fourteen feet up. My jaw dropped. Three radiant copper panels were already in place. Each art-deco style, two-foot square panel had a hand-pounded fan-shape in each corner and a diamond shape in the middle. An intricate hatch mark design decorated the background.

"Chester, they're beautiful!"

He smiled and turned on the little crystal lights. The total effect was breathtaking. He pointed to ten boxes of ten 24" x 24" antique copper squares. "It's a lot of work—ninety-four more panels and ninety-four more trips up the ladder, but it will be worth it."

I agreed. "Too bad the door is too narrow for a cherry-picker. That ladder work is a real killer! When are the Staley's coming home?"

"They think they'll be back tomorrow afternoon. I'll let you in tomorrow," he said, as he carried a copper panel eight feet up his ten-foot ladder. "Betty and Nibs are taking a few days off as well."

"Careful up there," I said, just before I turned the corner and walked down the hall to the mural. Alicia had already started work on the foreground, namely the beach. The darker wet sand began at the water's edge and became lighter as it moved down to the edge of the wainscoting. I painted glowing green waves dressed in white froth, breaking onto the beach that Alicia had just painted. I followed her, left to right, until our beach and waves finally made it twenty-four feet to the end of the mural.

"Allie, it's four o'clock—let's call it a day."

We cleaned brushes and arranged our gear against the wall. Chester stood by, ready to escort us out and to lock the doors. He looked exhausted. I was the first to drive away. Two streets later, I passed the cop's hiding place and looked in the rearview mirror. Sure enough, there was the front fender of his motorcycle. I laughed to myself, remembering how he had pulled me over— probably expecting to see a tough guy in the driver's seat.

I cruised through Aptos and over to Butler Street. After several knocks and a long wait, Clara answered the door at Denise's apartment. She wiped tears from her cheeks with a hanky.

"What's the matter, Auntie?"

"We're watching John Candy in *Only the Lonely.*" Clara pulled me inside, and we squeezed in next to Denise on the couch.

"Hi, Denise, having a good time?"

"Shhhh!" She leaned toward the big flat screen TV, tears running down her face.

At that point, John Candy had to decide between his overbearing mother and his sweetheart. We were all on edge, terrified that he might not choose the right woman. In fact, he did choose the wrong one.

Denise and Clara were outraged and shouted at the TV.

Even though I had seen the movie a couple of times and knew the ending, I couldn't help clenching my jaw whenever the mother, Maureen O'Hara, criticized the girlfriend, Ally Sheedy. Half an hour later, the happy ending happened, and Aunt Clara and Denise were ecstatic.

"How's your investigation going, Josephine?" Clara asked.

"I have a few suspects but nothing concrete."

"What are you working on, Josephine?" Denise asked.

"The Eddie Garrett murder," I said, feeling happy that she was finally taking an interest in something other than a movie. "I'm wondering about Eddie's neighbor. She sounded to me like Eddie was a typical case of unrequited love. And then there were these two guys at Eddie's house. They tried to scare me off. I took down their license plate number and gave it to Officer Sayer."

Denise looked impressed, but not enough to smile—almost excited enough to get back in uniform, but not quite.

"Okay, Auntie, are you ready to go home?"

"Yes, dear, but I'd like to come back tomorrow. Denise wants to take me to a wonderful restaurant in Capitola."

"I can drop you off in the morning and pick you up after work. That's a long day together; are you sure?"

Clara opened her mouth to say something.

"She's sure," Denise snapped. Yep, the old Denise was still around.

Driving Clara home was like all our rides together, chatty and fun. I asked her if she had learned what Denise's problem was.

Clara shook her head. "I have no idea what's bothering her. I just try to distract her and make her laugh. The poor girl looks like steel, but she bends with every disappointment."

"Like what? What makes her so sad and nasty?" I asked, as my little loaner car entered Highway One going south.

"She has no family, no husband, no children, but I think she's sweet on someone. She didn't say whom. Apparently he doesn't know she exists," Clara sighed. "I'll work on her again tomorrow."

After a quick stop at the grocery store to buy dog food, we headed southeast, in the direction of the tiny town of Aromas and my little adobe house. Sara and Solow were obviously glad to see us with his tail and her stub wagging energetically. Clara gave them some good lovin' while I went inside and checked the answering machine. There were two messages. The Body Shop had called to say I could pick up my truck. Chester called to say that the Staleys would be home tomorrow at ten o'clock in the morning to let us in, and he would be taking a day off because his mother was sick.

Chapter 7

Thursday morning I took my time getting ready for work. Aunt Clara was ready to go at dawn but forced herself to be quiet until seven-thirty. By that time, I was tired of listening to whispers and padding feet up and down the hallway. I heard the dogs go out the back door, heard them come in the front door, heard them chewing their kibble, heard Aunt Clara constantly telling them to be quiet, and I heard the perking coffee machine. Oh, the aroma!

"Josephine, you're up. The coffee's ready. Would you like some toast?"

"Yes, and peanut butter on the toast please."

Clara worked in the kitchen while I enjoyed a long hot shower. Life was good. The mural was, in Mr. Staley's words, "coming along nicely." I would get my truck back soon, Clara was helping Denise and I already had a couple of murder suspects in mind. I rinsed my hair and toweled off.

It was nine o'clock when Clara and I left Aromas. On our way to Aptos, we stopped in Watsonville at the Body Shop to trade in the purple Civic for my red Mazda pickup. Back on the highway, we sang to a song on the radio. Neither one of us knew how to sing worth a darn, but that was what made it so much fun. We were still laughing when I dropped Clara at Denise's.

Back on the road again, I cut across the highway to the ocean side of Aptos and eventually parked my truck behind Alicia's green Volvo SUV. And then it hit me—I hadn't called Alicia about the ten o'clock arrival time.

I peeked into Alicia's car. She was busy looking at pictures on her phone.

I tapped on the window.

Alicia looked at me, flipped through a few more pictures and finally climbed out of her car. "It's almost ten, where have you been?" she grumped.

"Sorry, Allie, I forgot to tell you that Chester isn't coming to work today. Oh, and the Staleys will be home by ten to let us in." We both looked around. No Maseratis anywhere.

She checked her watch and I checked mine.

"Allie, let's sit on the patio and watch the waves."

The two guys working on the roof watched us as we moseyed around the house and ended up on cushy seats with a five-star view of the pale blue ocean. The sun felt good on my skin. With summer on its way, a warm, contented feeling swept over me.

"Jo…ah, Jo, you can get up now," Alicia prodded. "Mr. Staley's at the door."

Startled into reality, I looked back at the French doors. Sure enough, Lloyd was staring at us from behind them. He opened one of the doors and greeted us, looking rested from the little trip he and Liana had taken. He even indulged in a bit of small talk for a change.

Suddenly a woman shrieked.

"What…in Sam Hill was that?" Lloyd exclaimed.

Clippity-clop shoes pounded down the hallway, getting louder.

"Lloyd, Lloyd…oh my God, there you are." Liana didn't say a word to her astonished muralists. Her face was contorted as she tried to tell Lloyd about something down the hall. She pointed toward the library as she choked on her words.

"Take a breath, dear," Lloyd said. But Liana didn't listen; she just tugged on her husband's sleeve, pulling him out of the room and down the hall.

Alicia and I stood frozen, like two flies stuck to a melted Hershey bar. Silence reigned until minutes later when the panicked couple came back to ask us a few questions. The main question urgently repeated several times by Liana who seemed to be on the verge of a breakdown was, "When was the last time you saw Chester?"

"He locked up the house yesterday a little after four o'clock," I said, feeling a weird sense of doom for young, capable, responsible Chester.

Alicia nodded, confirming what I had said, and the expression on her face reflecting my thoughts.

"Did you see him leave?" Lloyd asked.

I thought about it. "No, Alicia and I left about the same time, but I didn't see Chester come out of the house."

Alicia nodded, "I followed Josephine as far as the highway."

Lloyd helped his wife into a chair. She sat facing the ocean wearing a blank expression, her hands knitted together, shoulders collapsed.

"We have been robbed," Lloyd whispered. "Three-hundred thousand dollars' worth of copper panels...all gone—except for six of them already installed on the ceiling." His shoulders drooped worse than Liana's.

"The beautiful copper pan...oh, that's awful!" I groaned.

"Someone else did this, not Chester!" Alicia said emphatically.

I wanted to stand up and cheer. I should have said it. Alicia was right—Chester would never do anything like that. We knew what a great guy he was. But he did have *opportunity,* I thought, and then scolded myself for thinking such a terrible thing.

"Three-hundred thousand dollars?" I almost gagged on the figure. It was almost a third of the million-dollar remodel.

Liana nodded slowly, sadly, looking like a woman who had just been stabbed in the back by a trusted friend. She and Lloyd obviously had had great faith in Chester.

"Would you like us to go and leave you two alone...?" I asked.

"No, dear, we'll be fine," Liana said as she stood up, put her shoulders back and walked out of the room.

Lloyd followed her, but his shoulders were still caved.

Alicia and I worked in silence to the beat of the ever-crashing waves. To me they sounded like a sad heart struggling to survive in a world turned upside down. Why would someone take those lovely panels, and why would someone murder Eddie? But I knew the world didn't always make sense. All one had to do was watch the *Ten O'clock News* every night to know how many crazy things had happened that day.

"Allie, it's almost one. Let's take a lunch break."

"One minute, I just want to finish the last rock."

A few minutes later, the ocean, beach and boulders were finished. After lunch, we would paint an island off the coast. We gathered up our lunches and light jackets and strolled out to the patio. Below us, the tide was out and the waves were gentle...so inviting!

"Wouldn't it be wonderful to eat on the beach?" I said, moving closer to the edge of the patio. "There's a little path going down." I didn't wait for Alicia to answer. The call of the ocean was too strong to resist— so many memories of playing in the surf. Santa Cruz kids generally had those good times growing up. We body surfed during the foggy summer and played on the beach under a warm September sun, after the tourists left town.

My left hand gripped my little cooler, while the right hand slid along a wooden rail that slanted sharply down toward a tiny blue beach umbrella poked into the sand. A narrow, treacherous path had been carved into the side of the protruding landmass that served as a giant pedestal supporting the Staley Mansion. I imagined waves eroding three sides of the peninsula in a wintery, rainy high tide. Not a property for the timid investor.

A few crumbles of dirt hit my shoulders from above, letting me know that Alicia wasn't far behind. Parts of the path had steps cut into the cliff and other places just angled downward. But the end of the path didn't mean the beginning of sand. Not surprising, the last couple feet of steps had been washed out by high tides over the years. I let go of the railing and dropped down to the sand.

Alicia jumped down beside me.

"I was expecting warm sand," I said, shivering in my light jacket.

"It's only May," Alicia reminded me, not mentioning my stupid idea to have lunch on the beach.

We plowed through the sand a few yards to the large blue umbrella and sat down behind it, hiding ourselves from the offshore breeze. When lunch was finished, we looked around to see if there was another way back to the mansion. Yes, there was another way. Just walk a mile south, straight down the beach and hope there would be a way up to the road. Make a left on the road and walk a mile north. Or climb the path, which we did.

Sandy and wind-blown, we entered the Staley living room, breathing hard. The house was quiet. Even Herbert was absent. We discussed painting an island off the coast, rummaged through pictures of islands and finally decided we would use Santa Cruz Island because it had an interesting shape, rugged coastline, was partially green and because it was a favorite of the Staleys—anything to make them happy now that their beloved tiles were missing.

My calves cried out, "How can we support you and hold your body steady after that exhausting climb up the cliff?" Unfortunately painting murals is all about holding the body still while one steady hand moves the brush.

"Allie, I feel like I'm coming off of thirty hours of ladder work."

"I know what you mean, Jo; my legs are shaking, they're so tired. Maybe we should finish this tomorrow."

When the paints and such were organized and stowed against the wall, I notified Liana of our decision to leave early. She smiled weakly, looking thankful and ready to be alone.

Betty, always looking out for Liana, ushered us out the front door.

While walking to our vehicles, Alicia and I saw a familiar dark blue truck wearing a red smudge and a long silver scratch. Rod pulled the truck to a stop near the front entry to the house. Something was wrong with this picture. Rod strolled with attitude up to the Staley front door, and Chester wasn't even around.

Alicia waved to me and drove away. I followed her as far as the highway, then drove the back roads a few miles north to Denise's apartment building. Clara answered the door and immediately ran back to the sofa. She and Denise sniffled, wiped their eyes and stressed as they watched *Sleepless in Seattle* on the TV screen. I sat down and watched the movie for about the tenth time, since there was only about ten minutes of it left. Besides, I could see the ending a hundred times over and it wouldn't be enough.

Red-eyed, but up-lifted by the movie, Clara and I scrambled into my truck and took off for Eddie's place.

"Josephine, what exactly are we looking for when we get to Eddie's?"

"For one, I want to see what he had stashed in the basement, and maybe you could meet Eddie's neighbor. I'd like to know what you think of her."

Clara nodded contentedly, as she enjoyed the woodsy green areas and sunny meadows along Trout Gulch Road. I turned onto Trickle Creek, drove past Eddie's, up Bessie's driveway and parked behind her decades old Dodge pickup truck.

Bessie came out of the barn in a huff. "Oh, it's you again," she said. "Where's your little purple clown car?"

"It was a loaner. Looks like you have low pressure in this tire," I said, pointing to the right rear tire on her truck.

"So you came out here to tell me that?"

Clara stepped down from the passenger seat.

"Hello there, Ms. Hatch. So you're the nice lady Josephine told me about—and your lovely ranch." She did a full pivot in the gravel, admiring all views of the place. "She didn't tell me about your sweet yellow kitty," she said, bending at the waist to pet the elderly, shorthaired, cross-eyed cat. "Oh my, that made me a little dizzy." Clara teetered, and Bessie automatically stepped forward and grabbed her by the elbow.

"Call me Bessie."

"Thank you, dear. I think I need a glass of water if you don't mind."

"Come on up to the porch and sit down," Bessie said. She helped my aunt up the stairs and into a weathered wooden chair, totally ignoring me as she went to her kitchen to get a glass of water.

When Clara sipped the water, her eyes got big. "This is the sweetest most delicious water I've ever tasted!"

"Ah, yeah, it comes from my well," Bessie said, as she plopped down on the only other chair around.

I leaned against the porch rail and rolled my eyes at all the fuss over water that I didn't even get to taste.

Aunt Clara began telling Bessie her life story. When she finally got to her current and wonderful husband, Ben, she asked Bessie if she was married. Bessie shook her head and talked about inheriting the farm from her parents, so why would she want a husband. Although she did adopt and raise her nephew, Brody Hatch, after her sister died.

A horse whinnied.

Bessie automatically turned her head toward a big red barn, situated about a hundred feet from the house.

"Was that a horse?" Clara asked.

"Two horses. I was hoping to breed them, but it's been two years and nothing's happened."

"That's too bad, dear; a little colt would be fun," Clara giggled. "Well, I suppose we should run along." She didn't look a bit dizzy as she stood up, and straightened her long flower-print blouse over her black yoga pants. Clara held onto my arm going down the five rickety steps but not because she needed to. She waved goodbye to Bessie, and we climbed into my truck. I turned the truck around slowly and looked back at Bessie's house. A curtain moved in the attic window above the porch.

A minute later, we were parked on the side of the road halfway to Eddie's driveway.

"I need a good walk, Auntie. Are you up for one?"

"Certainly, dear, I spent most of my day watching TV. I could use a good stretch of the legs."

Clara and I stopped at the faded, hand-printed Trickle Creek sign to catch our breath. From there, it was all downhill to Eddie's house. We crossed over the tiny crystal clear flow of spring water and headed down to the house. I checked under the front door welcome mat for a key. No key. We searched a potted geranium with no luck. I circled the house looking for a potential window, but they were all locked. Finally, I followed Clara down a steep dirt path that went directly to a basement built into the hillside under the house.

The door was ajar.

"Careful, Auntie...."

She charged through the doorway and switched on a light.

We looked around at the stacks of new five-gallon paint cans and a floor-to-ceiling pile of sheets of plywood and wallboard. Dozens of new tools still in their original boxes lined two walls, six feet high, and buckets of new paint brushes and cardboard boxes full of hammers, chisels, nail guns and spray kits lined a third wall. Dozens of shiny new rakes, shovels and hoes leaned in an orderly fashion against the fourth wall. Three shiny new generators sat in one corner.

"Clara, look up there, a door. Must be the steps up to the house. What do you think?"

"As long as we're here, we might as well take a look," she said, climbing up the stairs to the kitchen. I followed Clara into the kitchen and through several other rooms. We wandered through two small tidy bedrooms, and then into a third bedroom turned into a junk room full of boxes of plumbing fixtures, brand new door knobs, hinges, electrical boxes, alarm systems and so on.

"Oh, Eddie! Why did you let someone do this? I have a feeling someone was taking advantage of Eddie, taking over his home," Clara groaned. "Josephine, did you hear something?"

"I think I heard doors slamming, like on a car or a truck." I ran to the front window. "Dang, those guys I told you about are coming down to the house."

Without another word, we pounded down the stairs to the basement closing the kitchen door behind us. I hurried to the outside door, pulled it closed and locked it. Quickly we dragged several heavy boxes of tools over to the door, wedging them between the pile of wallboard and the door. We rolled all three generators over to the pile and stacked some large tools on top of the boxes for good measure. We reached as high as we could, building a heavy wall of junk between them and us.

I turned out the light.

Huddling in the dark, we listened to men thumping down the path.

Chapter 8

I held my breath forever, it seemed. Aunt Clara and I shivered in absolute darkness, except for the tiniest sliver of daylight seeping under Eddie's basement door. We listened to a key working the lock, some strong language and an occasional boot-kick on the door when the knob turned, but the door wouldn't open. The only thing between the burglars and us was a giant load of hardware.

Finally, footsteps retreated. All was quiet, until we heard pounding and kicking on the front door. My heart raced until we realized the basement key didn't work on the front door. If it had worked, the men wouldn't be kicking the door. But there were plenty of windows to break. Apparently, the men were not willing to trash the house. Obviously, they were no strangers to Eddie's basement. Maybe they didn't want to call attention to that fact.

My Aunt and I sighed, as doors slammed and a pickup truck roared away. All was quiet. I flipped the light switch and we climbed the stairs up to the kitchen.

"I'm thirsty," Aunt Clara said as she opened several cupboard doors and finally found a neat row of glasses. She filled one with tap water, sipped and said, "This water is just as good as Bessie's."

"Seriously?" I said.

"Yes, I believe it is, but Eddie has spring water...."

"Yeah," I rubbed my chin. "I don't think Bessie's water comes from a well. All the well water I've ever tasted was nothing to brag about." Why would she lie about her water?

We decided to sit at the kitchen table for a minute until our nerves settled. Staring at Eddie's dirty breakfast plate and an empty beer bottle left on the table from the day he died put a cloud of sadness over me. I was sure that Clara felt the same way.

"It's not a very sunny house, is it?" Clara said, between sips of delicious water.

"Speaking of houses and sad things, you'll never guess what happened at the Staley Mansion." I told my aunt the whole story because I knew she wouldn't tell anyone. Even though Chester had asked me not to tell a soul, I began with Chester showing me the secret stairways in the library and ending with Rod showing up as if he were there to save the day. Just thinking about him put a terrible taste in my mouth.

"This guy, Rod, isn't he the one who ran into your truck?"

"Yep, never even took the red paint off his fender. And Chester didn't have anything good to say about him either."

"Do you think Chester took the panels?" she asked.

"No, he would never, ever do anything like that. But it really looks bad for him since he was the last person to leave the mansion, as far as we know." I wished I knew a way to help Chester.

We heard a key in the front door lock.

"Did you hear that?" Clara whispered.

"Yeah," I said, as I grabbed the beer bottle, crept across the kitchen and peeked around the corner just as the front door opened. It was too late to run, especially since the only other way out was through the basement, and that door had some major blockage in front of it.

"Josie?"

"David, what are you doing here?"

"Jimmy and I are taking turns checking on the house. Today is my turn. What's the beer bottle for?"

"Well, you just missed the burglars. They tried to get in a while ago, but Aunt Clara and I held them off. We thought they were coming back." I sunk into his arms, feeling safe at last.

Clara walked into the room. "Well, what do ya know, it's David." She smiled, probably feeling safe for the first time since Mustache and Big Belly arrived.

"How did you two get here...I didn't see your truck?" David asked.

"We felt like walking, so I parked it up the road—halfway to Bessie's."

"And Bessie is...?"

"The neighbor who went looking for her cat and found Eddie," Clara said.

Tired and hungry, we quickly decided that we should all head home right away. David said he wanted to know more about the so-called burglars and would bring it up again when we came to his house for dinner. We piled into his Jeep, and he delivered us up the road to my truck.

"Dinner's at seven, and Fiona and Jimmy are coming," he hollered out his window and sped away.

Clara and I climbed into our seats and I fired up the engine. We had careened around two sharp turns in the road when I glimpsed a familiar looking white Chevy pickup with over-sized tires and fancy rims parked at the end of a short driveway.

"Did you see that?" I asked.

Clara looked right and left. "See what?"

"I think I just saw the burglars' truck. I wonder if they live around here or they're just waiting for us to leave."

"They're not very pleasant," Clara huffed, as we sped along Trout Gulch toward Highway One. It was five-thirty in the afternoon with commute traffic in full swing. Clara dropped her head back and closed her eyes. We chugged along the highway averaging twenty-two miles per hour. She opened her eyes when the truck finally pulled to a stop in front of my house. We had twenty minutes to feed the dogs and make ourselves presentable for dinner.

Aunt Clara fed the dogs while I took a quick shower to get the sand out of my hair and paint off my hands and arms.

Clara knocked on the bathroom door.

"I'll be out in a min..."

"Dear, Officer Sayer is on the phone."

"One minute—I'll be right there." I hung up the towel and slipped into my robe.

"Well, don't you look shiny clean!" Clara said as she handed me the house phone.

"Hello."

"Ms. Stuart, this is Sergeant Sayer. I have a couple quick questions to ask you."

"Sure, fire away." Water drizzled down my forehead from sopping wet hair.

"Do you know the whereabouts of a Chester Mathus?"

"No, I don't even know where he lives," I said.

"When was the last time you saw him?"

"Wednesday after work at the Staley house. He walked Alicia and me outside."

"Did you see him drive away from the Staley home?"

"No, and I think you're on the wrong track. There's a guy working there, Rod, who's a real creep..."

"Thank you, Ms. Stuart. We'll be in touch." Sayer hung up.

That was funny. I thought he said "we," as if he's still working with Officer Lund. Did Sayer get a new partner? Would Denise snap out of her problem, whatever it was, and go back to work? I used the hairdryer on my hair, a bit of light makeup and quickly scraped various colors of paint out from under my fingernails. My green blouse and black slacks would have to do, along with sandals and faux emerald earrings.

Clara and I grabbed sweaters and purses and traipsed down my driveway and up David's, with Sara and Solow in the lead. It was almost seven-thirty, and Jimmy and his wife had not arrived yet.

David welcomed us into his house.

"What's that heavenly smell," Clara swooned.

"I think you're smelling the apricot pie...."

"You made an apricot pie? Did you know that's my favorite?" she asked.

"I hope you like this one," he said, modestly.

"You'll love it Auntie! He picks the apricots, dries them and reconstitutes them to make pies all year long."

"Lovely! Oh look," she said pointing out the dining room window. "What is that beautiful red car?"

"Jimmy's Lamborghini," David yelled from the kitchen. "Actually, I think it's Fiona's car."

"Red!" I drooled. We stayed at the dining room window watching the couple exit that amazing car. Fashion was never my "thing," but I was always impressed when I saw it. And Fiona had "it" in spades. She looked elegant in her cerulean blue silk dress and silver accessories. Her dark curls were stacked jauntily on top of her head. She looked very petite next to her husband. I wondered if he had dressed up on his own, or had Fiona laid out his clothes and told him which pair of shoes to wear? I forced myself to put aside all the things I had heard about the woman, hoping to make a fresh judgment.

Clara hurried outside to greet the couple.

David fussed around in the kitchen, pulling his pie out of the oven.

Watching from the window, I saw Clara introduce herself. Jimmy gave my aunt a hug, and then Fiona gave her air kisses. My mind shot into the future, where David and I were married and Jimmy and Fiona were our best friends. Every time we went anywhere with them, I would have to dress up; but I would never look "put-together" like Fiona. And I would have to suffer any number of phony air kisses. After that little daydream, I almost lost my appetite, but not quite. The pie smelled so good!

Once David made the introductions and more air kisses were blown, I made myself busy setting the dining room table. I found the old wine bottles with drippy candles stuck in the tops. They weren't ascetically copacetic with the plates and tablecloth. Maybe that was why I chose them. Or maybe I did it because of the memories attached to those old bottles.

Fiona practically wet her pants when she saw the candles. "Jim, isn't that the cutest thing? So 'Tuscany country-casual.' I just love the theme, Josephine. I heard that you are way into artsy motifs." She smiled and blinked her long lashes expressively.

It was all I could do to keep from shoving a finger down my throat.

"Actually, I make my living as a muralist—you know, someone who paints pretty pictures on walls," I said.

"I know what a muralist is. I was involved in the grant process for the murals in the San Jose City Hall." She turned and followed Clara to the living room and took a seat on the couch. My aunt had a lot more patience with Fiona than I. Pretty soon they were doubled over with laughter. Even Solow and Sara loved being with them.

Luckily, the men didn't give a darn about petty feelings. They went about their kitchen business, taking occasional trips to the barbecue in the back yard where they could talk and laugh freely.

I lit the Tuscany country-casual candles, tossed dressing into a big green salad and filled all the glasses with cucumber water. Feeling left out of the men's conversation and the women's, I realized I had made myself the "fifth wheel" of the party. Maybe I should reconsider my annoyance with air kisses. Maybe they were a sign of good intentions. And maybe pigs could fly. The evening had just begun. It could get better or it could bomb. It was David's event, and it was up to me to step on my pride and try to make the dinner party a success.

An hour later, one lonely slice of tri-tip, a baked potato and two spears of asparagus were the only remnants of a delicious dinner. We had eaten all of the salad, the bread and the apricot pie à la mode. The guys planned to clean up the kitchen and told the women to relax in the living room.

We girls, except for Sara, had made ourselves comfortable on the couch watching a men's beach volleyball tournament on TV.

There was a commotion in the kitchen.

David yelled for us to "do something!"

Clara and I ran into the kitchen.

"Oh, Sara," Clara cried as she got down on her knees and bent over Sara. The poor dog's eyes were rolling around as she made gagging noises. She lay on her side, her feet twitching like mad.

"I gave her the last piece of meat," David confessed. "The whole slice went down...."

"Oh, dear," Clara whimpered.

Suddenly I remembered seeing a similar situation in a TV program about pit bulls.

"David, stand her up! Now, pick up Sara's back legs," I shouted, knowing I would not be able to lift the back half of a full-grown Rottie.

He hesitated for a second, saw the logic of it and picked up the legs.

"Raise them up as high as you can," I begged.

He raised her back legs but nothing came out of Sara's mouth. While the legs were up, I worked my hand into Sara's mouth. I couldn't feel the meat. It was time for a more drastic measure.

"Oh Sara!" Clara cried, petting her dog's frightened furry face.

"David, keep her legs up. I'm going to do a Heimlich maneuver on her." I leaned the left side of my body against Sara's right hip, wrapped my left arm over her backside and my right arm went under her belly. My hands came together in a single fist, which I aimed at the soft belly just below her rib cage. I used more force on the second try and even more on the third.

Sara heaved and out popped the slab of barbecued beef.

When David set her back legs down, she looked at us as if to say, "What's all the fuss?"

Clara bent at the waist to pick up the slimy piece of meat before Sarah could try to eat it again.

Jimmy caught Aunt Clara as she headed for the floor.

"Thank you, Jimmy."

He helped her into a chair at the kitchen table, while David picked up the meat. Clara was all smiles and tears as she trembled from head to toe. But once she caught her breath, she was at Sara's side giving her buckets of love. She thanked David and me profusely for saving Sara's life.

"Clara, why did you adopt such a large dog?" Fiona asked, when my aunt and I finally joined her on the couch.

"Sara was looking for a home and she chose me, and I will always be thankful."

"Jimmy and I thought about having a pet, but we could never decide what it would be," Fiona said, "you know, cat, dog, turtle."

"That's great, it leaves you open for lots of travel," Clara said.

"Not really—boats make Jimmy seasick and I refuse to fly." She flicked an invisible particle of dust off her lap.

"How about trains?"

She wrinkled her nose, "Just too boring."

Fiona's whole life sounded boring to me. It sounded like all she did was play tennis and have her nails and hair done. No career, no worries! I fell for all the boring details of her life, but Aunt Clara was able to peel the onion and discover what Fiona was really about. Fiona said she spent time everyday helping to take care of her ailing mother; she also wrote a book called *Love It Or Trash It* that dealt with hoarding, and she was on the San Jose City Council.

"So, Fiona, what do you think about Eddie getting murdered?" I asked.

She studied her perfect thumbnail. "It could be follow the money or follow the water, but it might have been a confrontation with a stranger," she shrugged. "I've never been to Eddie's house, and he only came to our house once in the last twenty years."

I wondered if he had ever been invited.

"Eddie kept his house very neat and clean," I said, and Clara nodded.

David and Jimmy entered the room, bragging and laughing about how clean the kitchen looked and how abused they were by their women. Clara and I thought that was funny—but there was no "funny" on Fiona's face.

I was still thinking about Eddie's neat and clean house, except for the dirty plate and empty beer bottle left on the kitchen table. At least I knew that David didn't want to marry me for my housekeeping skills, since his were much better than mine.

Later that night I dreamt I had to go to a formal function with David and the Garrett's. Fiona wore a dress that consisted of layers of ruffles made from my kitchen curtains. She wore several colorful bracelets on her wrists and Solow's collar around her neck. I planned to wear my faux diamond necklace and my engagement ring because everyone seemed to be so interested in them. Maybe that was because I had remembered to wear the necklace and the ring, but forgot everything else. Fiona commented on my sense of fashion simplicity, as in "no clothes."

Chapter 9

Friday morning I woke up early but stayed in bed for a while thinking about the night before. Dinner at David's had been a bit trying for me, but eventually I joined the fun. I learned that Fiona had some substance to her, things to admire, but not much I could relate to. She ate nothing but salad and trashed Eddie at every opportunity. It was like she had a permanent burr under her saddle.

Jimmy put on a poker face early in the evening and kept it there, except for some relaxing time spent at the backyard barbecue with David.

Climbing out of bed, I heard Aunt Clara coming down the hall. She tapped on my door. I opened it.

"Auntie, you're still in your robe," I laughed. She wore a long flannel nightgown under her fluffy pink robe. Normally she would be dressed and ready to go very early.

"It's silly, but I slept in," Clara giggled. "I think I was so relieved to have my dear Sara alive and well, I just slept like the dead. How did you sleep, dear?"

"My dreams were even more weird than the dinner party," I laughed.

"Did you notice that giant diamond on Fiona's finger?" Clara said.

"Notice it, I was blinded by it. But I can't imagine her wearing anything smaller. It would diminish her whole station in life."

"Now, Josephine, she's different but I'm sure Fiona is a good person at heart," Clara said.

"If she has a heart," I mumbled to myself.

We trundled down the hall to the kitchen where Mr. Coffee did his morning duty. From there, I shuffled down the driveway in my robe and slippers and retrieved the newspaper. Back in the house, Clara and I sipped our coffee. I thumbed through the paper and found nothing pertaining to the theft of nearly a hundred very expensive copper panels. Had the Staleys not reported them missing or did they somehow manage to keep the story out of the paper?

"Josephine, if you don't mind, I'd like to go with you again this morning."

"Sure, Auntie, I was counting on it. You and Denise seem to hit it off pretty well."

"Denise left a message on the answering machine. She wanted to watch *The African Queen* with me. I've seen the movie a few times already, but one more won't hurt," she chuckled.

An hour later, our morning routine, including breakfast, had been completed. Clara and I piled into my truck. It was a beautiful sunny morning, and I looked forward to finishing the ocean mural and possibly starting the dining room mural. But I dreaded running into Rod. I pictured him at home in bed with a thermometer in his mouth and red splotches all over his body. If I had owned a Rod doll, I would have poked it with a hundred pins.

Clara was quiet, probably thinking of more ways to make Denise happy and bring out her personality—or give her one. I dropped my aunt at the apartment and then backtracked over to the Seascape area of Aptos. Just one block from the Staley Mansion, I spotted a white Ford 150 with a mega toolbox parked at the curb. I slowed down for a closer look, and sure enough, it was Chester's truck with Chester in it. I parked at the curb, got out and walked up to his window.

"I was hoping you'd stop, Josephine. I wanted to tell you not to worry...."

"What do you mean, don't worry? I've been worried sick about you. Did you know that the panels are gone? And the Staleys think you took them!"

"That's what I'm talkin' about—don't worry, things aren't the way they look." Chester started his truck engine and slipped it into gear.

"Wait, Chester; I know you didn't do it. But who did?" I shouted as he backed up, pulled away from the curb and drove out of the neighborhood. Stomping my feet didn't help to release my frustration.

An old woman walking her two little dogs looked the other way, probably stifling a good laugh.

It seemed like everywhere I went there was murder and theft going on. Were any of the problems connected? Back in my truck, I drove one block, turned right and down the Staley driveway. Mentally preparing myself for another day of "never a dull," I realized that even Alicia was not as perky and positive as usual. Maybe the Staleys' problems were getting to her too. I climbed out of my truck and joined Alicia at the grand entrance.

Liana saw us coming and opened the door.

"Lovely day, isn't it?" Liana exclaimed, looking like sunshine itself—if sunshine was a liar. She was overdoing the stiff upper lip routine.

We agreed that it was a beautiful day. *How could it be anything else when the ocean was just a stone's throw away*, I thought.

We tried to be as enthusiastic as Liana about our work, even after we found a list of items to be added to the painting. The note was posted on the mural wall and mentioned sailboats on the water, seagulls in the sky and umbrellas on the beach.

"Someday I want to just paint something different, like a great white shark," I said, gazing out the glass doors at the real ocean. The water was deep ultramarine blue with a purple cast along the horizon, and the sandy waves were huge and mesmerizing. Reluctantly I left that glorious sight and returned to the mural.

Alicia cleared her throat a couple of times.

I looked up from my palette.

Liana stood in the doorway. "Is the list okay?" she asked.

"Absolutely," I said, just before she turned and walked away. Fortunately, I had prepared a folder full of magazine pictures of sea birds, turtles, islands and a host of other subjects we might be asked to paint. Adding an island, boats, gulls and umbrellas was like telling a story. The gulls circled in the air, five far-away little fishing boats were making their way back to a safe harbor and there were only three umbrellas left on the beach, all because a storm was on its way. Alicia saw it the other way around. The gulls, the people with umbrellas and the fishing boats were all headed out, now that the storm was over.

"I saw Chester today," I said quietly.

"You saw..."

"Shhhh!" I whispered, looking to make sure we were alone. "I saw Chester this morning, right here in this neighborhood. He told me that things aren't like they appear, but I don't know what that means."

"The facts as we know them..." Alicia said, "are that the panels are missing, and Chester was the last person to leave the mansion."

"Maybe he wasn't the last one to leave," I said from halfway up the six-foot ladder. I dabbed wings onto a soaring seagull and leaned to my right to create another bird, while Alicia painted colorful little umbrellas on the beach.

"Liana seems to be dealing with it much better today," Alicia said.

"Yeah, I'm wondering about that. If I just lost something worth three-hundred-thousand dollars, I would be in a bad mood for a very long time." Reflecting on it, I decided the most valuable thing I owned was Solow. Or did he own me?

"Jo, isn't that your phone?"

"Yeah," I said, as I put the painty end of my brush into a plastic sandwich bag and then rummaged through my purse for the phone. "Hello?"

"Josephine, dear, I hope I'm not interrupting anything…"

"No, Auntie, don't worry; I'm taking a little break. What can I do for you?"

"Denise and I just finished watching *The African Queen*, and now we're going through Netflix trying to decide between *Titanic* and *Uncle Buck*."

"Well, they're both wonderful movies. Do you want to laugh or cry?"

"We've done a lot of crying. I think laughing would be good," Aunt Clara said.

"I think you would enjoy *Uncle Buck*—a little bit of tears and lots of laughs. Is there any chance you guys can get outside for a walk?"

"Not yet," Clara said, "but I'm working on it. Thank you, dear." She hung up.

Alicia walked over to the glass doors where I stood gazing at the ocean.

"Jo, how can you compare *Titanic* to *Uncle Buck*?"

"Actually, I was comparing emotions. Besides, a good movie is a good movie whether it's a huge production or just a good story done well. Let's finish this mural and then go to lunch. I'd like to try out the little Mexican place down the road."

By one o'clock, we were putting the finishing touches (white caps) on the ocean, and a bit more shadowing under the waves. In unison, we stepped back and studied the full effect.

"Done! Let's go to lunch," I said, as we cleaned our brushes. Alicia pulled off the masking tape while I tidied up the area.

"Jo, have you seen the Staleys' cat today?"

I thought about it. "No, I haven't. That's strange; Herbert's usually trying to wrap his body around my ankles."

As we walked through the house, I pulled Alicia toward the library, wanting to show her the half dozen copper panels on the ceiling.

She looked up. "Wow, the panels are beautiful. How sad that the rest of them are missing." While she inspected the beautiful room, I walked over to an antique carved-wood desk. The desktop and drawers were empty. I bent down and checked the wastebasket. At first look, it appeared to be empty. But a postage stamp-sized piece of paper was stuck to the bottom. I retrieved the little piece of paper and tucked it into my pocket as I followed Alicia out the door. Part of me wanted to show her the secret staircases. I wondered if the Staleys knew about them.

Once we were sitting at a table in the Mexican restaurant, I pulled out the little torn square of paper. It seemed to be the only remains of a hand-printed letter: "will kill your ca." I shuffled the words and half words around in my head as we finished our tostadas and iced tea. It was two-thirty when we arrived back at the Staley house.

"Jo, are you going to show me that little piece of paper?" Alicia asked as we sat in my truck.

"What paper? Oh, that…sure." I hadn't planned to show it to her because she always made such a fuss about my nosing into people's business, but I handed it over.

Alicia laughed when she saw the paper. "Well, that's easy to read. Rust will kill your carburetor," she laughed. "Or, hiking will kill your calves. How about, my cat will kill your canary?"

"Hungry wolves will kill your cattle," I offered.

"Exercise will kill your calories," she suggested.

"I will kill your cat." Even as I joked, suddenly I imagined someone threatening to kill Herbert. What monster would threaten such a thing?

"Jo, that's not funny!"

"I'm not trying to be funny. I'm trying to figure out what this torn up note was about…a note that happened to be in the same room as the missing copper panels. Obviously someone dumped the trash, and one little piece of a torn up note refused to leave the bin."

"You think that's a clue…?"

"Clues are where you find them," I smiled.

Alicia rolled her eyes and climbed out of the truck.

Liana opened the front door just as we started up the front steps. She looked as put-together perfect as ever, except for an unsettled look in her gray-green eyes…as if she felt a huge sadness but couldn't talk about it.

Alicia and I moved the tarps, ladders and paint into the dining room where we would again be painting above the wainscoting. The subject would be our impression of Edward Hopper's famous "Chop Suey" painting from 1920. We planned to copy the painting, generally, of two women sitting at a table in a Chinese restaurant. To fill the seventeen-foot-long wall, we would simply add more tables and people. The twenties style, using strong colors, would lend itself nicely to the transformation of the Staley Mansion as it headed back to its original Arts and Crafts period.

"Allie, have you seen Herbert?"

"No, why are you so worried about...oh, you really do think the note was about him?"

"It could be," I said, and left it at that because there were so many details to consider in the Hopper mural. I needed to concentrate. Using two-foot-long levels, we made chalk lines for ten windows. Working from right to left, the first two windows angled into the picture, while eight more windows were lined up two feet above the wainscot and rose five feet up to the ceiling. Alicia finished drawing the last three windows, and I mixed up three shades of a gray-blue.

As always, we painted whatever was furthest away first, in this case, the sky outside the windows. We needed to start at the top of each window and work down, but I had only brought one ladder. Alicia knew the drill and went to work on the window furthest to the left, applying a swath of the darkest blue from the crown molding downward. Quickly she switched to the second darkest shade and blended it into the first. Then came the lightest shade that was very light and had a touch of yellow in it—a touch of dirty-city sunshine. The last color was blended and ended three feet above the wainscoting.

Unable to find the Staleys or anyone else in the house, I ventured outside to look around. The only two people working on the grounds were Rod and his hired man, José. Rod was giving the hedges an uneven trim as José hauled the cuttings over to an open-top wooden trailer attached to the back of Rod's pickup. I approached José hoping I wouldn't have to talk to Rod.

"José," I said, standing in his path, "do you have a ladder I can borrow?"

Rod's trimmer went quiet.

José looked over his shoulder at Rod and then back to me. "Go to the back of the house. When you go inside there's a green door on your right. It goes to a storage room...."

"Shut up, José, and get to work!" Rod yelled.

Chin up and shoulders squared, I headed for the green door. José was right. Instead of taking the steps up to the laundry room, I opened the green door to my right. Instantly I was hit with a strong oily shop smell, reminding me of David's workbench in his garage. Amongst a large assortment of tools and hardware, I found a six-foot aluminum ladder and hauled it up to the laundry room. While admiring the spotless utility room, I noticed that Herbert's food and water bowls were missing.

I continued down the hall and placed the ladder in front of the mural.

Using a three-inch-wide brush, Alicia swiftly painted the last half of the second window. The two painted rectangles looked identical, and she hadn't even broken a sweat.

My first window was the one on the far right side of the wall. I painted and blended like mad. Around four-thirty, Alicia and I met in the middle of the wall. We were feeling tired but happy to have the first layer of the painting, the sky, finished. It was a good stopping place, so we cleaned brushes, organized our stuff against the wall and said goodbye to Liana.

Alicia headed home to Watsonville while I drove north across Aptos to Denise's apartment. Clara opened the door for me, looking like she just woke up from a nap. Denise opened her eyes and looked up sleepily from her seat on the sofa.

"Looks like you two had a nap," I said, stating the obvious as I gathered up my aunt's purse and sweater. "How was today's movie?"

Clara laughed, "I thought Denise was going to drown herself in tears when Margaret Sullivan found out that her secret pen pal was Jimmy Stewart. Actually, it was quite a moment. Have you seen *The Shop Around the Corner*?"

"David and I watched the movie on TV about a year ago. He's a big fan of old movies. I'm okay with them." I remembered how his eyes had glistened at the end. He was just one big romantic Teddy bear.

"Josephine," Denise yawned, "you'll be happy to know that we took a walk today."

"I noticed you're getting some color in your cheeks, Denise."

"I'm feeling better, thanks to your Aunt Clara. Would you mind taking me to the crime scene?"

"Eddie's? Now?" I gulped, as my body cried out for rest after a long day of painting.

"Well, if it's not convenient...."

"That's okay, grab your purse and let's go," I said, not wanting to slow the momentum of the woman's progress. The three of us piled into the cab of my pickup. Tall, skinny Denise sat on the console between the bucket seats. Clara and I stuffed our Rubenesque bodies into our tight little window seats. We slammed our doors, I turned the key, and we moved slowly through the neighborhood. At the first stop sign, my right foot got tangled up with Denise's foot, causing us to stop on top of the crosswalk instead of behind it.

Red lights zoomed up behind us. A loudspeaker system told me to move my vehicle to the curb.

Chapter 10

Red-faced and wishing I could crawl into the nearest pot hole, I looked up at the officer who looked very familiar. I remembered his brown eyes, the tone of his voice and his shiny motorcycle helmet. He leaned down, looked at the three of us and asked to see my license.

Clara felt around the floor for my purse and eventually handed me my wallet. I took out my driver's license and handed it to the officer.

"New set of wheels?" he asked, with a tinge of sarcasm.

"Old set," I said.

"Where's your seatbelt, ma'am?" he asked Denise, who looked straight ahead, the top of her head smooshed against the ceiling.

"There isn't a belt in the middle," I explained, as if that would solve the problem. Actually, I wasn't worried. I had a *bonafide* Santa Cruz County Sheriff sitting right next to me. Besides, we were wedged in shoulder-to-shoulder. There was no way Denise could be thrown anywhere.

But Denise didn't say a word.

I felt my face turning red.

"We're taking our friend to Dominical Hospital," Clara said. "She, ah, fell and hurt her ankle. It might be broken."

On cue, (a push from Clara's knee) Denise grimaced.

"Are you all right, ma'am?" the officer asked.

Denise nodded bravely, sucked in some air, then let her chin rest on her chest with her eyes closed.

"She'll be okay as soon as we get her to a doctor," Clara said. "She's feeling rather puny so we need to hurry."

The officer handed me my license and let us go on the condition that we go straight to the hospital and never go without a seatbelt again.

Three blocks down the road, we lost the motorcycle. Feeling like the pressure was off, I finally released a nervous giggle. Pretty soon, we were all giggling. That turned into laughter, as we made a couple of left turns and headed for Trout Gulch Road instead of the hospital. When we finally arrived at Eddie's place, the sun had dropped behind the trees, dropping the temperature from comfortable to need-a-sweater. We climbed out of the cab like three clowns exiting a Minnie Mouse car.

Denise was all business, wanting to know what had happened and where. She gazed into the Trickle Creek spring water, dipped both hands into it and drank. Shaking her head, she said, "Good, except for a slight taste of gun oil. From there, she walked over to the twenty-foot-long stack of firewood bordering one side of the driveway. She studied the length of it, pushed an empty apple crate against the pile and stepped up onto it. She pondered the long flat top of the neatly stacked oak in dimming daylight, and finally stepped down without a word.

"See anything up there?" Clara asked.

"Someone has been taking wood from the stack recently. Maybe even today." Denise studied the unpaved driveway, and followed a size eleven tennis shoe impression about ten feet until it disappeared. My aunt and I were impressed, to say the least. Maybe Denise had always been the "brains" of her partnership with Officer Sayer, and he was the people person—the one who tells people not to jump off the bridge or shoot the hostage. Denise would probably have the opposite effect on her suicidal subject.

As a group, we clambered down the wooden runway and veered onto the steep dirt path leading to the basement.

"Oh my!" Aunt Clara exclaimed.

"Jeese Louise," Denise said.

"What in the…?" I groaned. "Looks like someone took an ax to this door."

"No," Denise said. "I think it was a Saws-all and a hammer. See the marks on the doorknob? First they beat the doorknob with the hammer, then they got the saw and cut this hole big enough to crawl through. Obviously, the boxes and piles of stuff stopped them from going inside."

Clara and I looked at each other and smiled.

"We put that stuff there," Clara said. "You'd be surprised how much you can do when the adrenaline kicks in. We had buckets of adrenaline going for us!"

Denise looked at us with new respect. "I see what we're up against here, probably a thief—at least a hoarder. Has Officer Sayer seen this?"

Clara shook her head. "I don't think so."

Slack-jawed, we gazed at the destruction.

I felt a bit dazed as we hiked up to the driveway. Suddenly we heard the roar of an engine and were shocked to see a white pickup truck with snazzy gold rims backing up, turning around and speeding up the driveway to the road. Even though they had a head start on us, we piled into my truck, pushing and groaning until the doors were finally able to close. I put my truck in reverse and backed up twenty feet, put it in drive, cranked the wheel to the right and drove another hundred yards up to the road. We turned right and I punched it.

"Careful, Josephine," Clara cautioned.

"Step on it!" Denise ordered.

My truck bounced and shook as we sped along the curvy Trout Gulch Road. Shoulder to shoulder like a pickle sandwich, the three of us bounced in unison until we finally jerked to a stop at Freedom Boulevard. We hadn't seen a white pickup yet, so we voted two to one to turn right on Freedom. We hung a right and cruised north through Aptos Village.

"I'm starving!" the pickle said, as if she were a normal, red-blooded American with an actual appetite, not the stiff policewoman we had known.

"Me too!" Clara chimed in, because she always was close to being normal.

My very normal tummy told me I was hungry too. We all agreed that tacos would fill the bill, so we visited the first taqueria we came across. The teenager behind the counter looked at my rainbow outfit with admiration. Running my hand over my multi-colored t-shirt, I explained that I was a painter. She smiled smugly, probably comparing her many exotic tattoos to my primitive paint smudges.

Ms. Tattoos set up our table with a basket of corn chips, a bowl of guacamole and a bowl of salsa. Each of us did our part to get to the bottom of the bowls. Aunt Clara ended up with a bit of green guacamole on the front of her blouse. When I told her about it, she pointed out the salsa on my shirt. Denise was a more careful eater, but fast. It seemed like the Sheriff was working on all new batteries— thanks to my Aunt Clara.

Just as the tacos and burritos arrived, I happened to look out the window facing the Chicken Place across the street. A white pickup with fancy rims was parked there.

"Hey, you two, look!" I stood up and pointed out the window.

Denise and Aunt Clara turned in their seats to look.

"It's them!" Clara stammered.

"They're leaving with a bag of chicken," Denise scowled. "The large economy size."

"Auntie, stay with the food—we'll be back."

Denise and I ran through a flood of teenage girl soccer players pouring through the front entrance. With lots of "excuse me's," we made it out the door, across the parking lot and across the street in time to smell a puff of diesel exhaust from the white truck as it rumbled away.

"It's probably just as well," I said, "you don't even have a gun."

"I would have questioned them, at least." Sheriff Lund looked disappointed. "I'm pretty good in the martial arts, you know."

"Which one?"

"All of them. It's my hobby. Are you surprised?"

"Well, I figured it wouldn't be knitting."

Back at the taqueria, we found Clara sitting at a table surrounded by sweaty, talkative teenage girls. She had their attention as she told all she knew about the murder committed on Trout Gulch Road. She asked for their help in finding two men, one heavy and one sporting a black mustache, driving a white truck with fancy tire rims and a green RECYCLE bumper sticker.

Our food was served. It tasted like comfort food times ten. When we had finished eating, I dug through my purse and came up with business cards for the whole soccer team.

"Call me if you see these guys." I said. "One guy has a big belly and the other one…"

A girl next to me interrupted, "Don't worry, we got it all from Aunt Clara."

They lined up for a hug from my aunt, as we worked our way to the door. For a woman who never had children of her own, Clara had always had a way with young people, and people in general.

As we filed out the door, one girl commented to Denise, "Are you wearing contacts…or are your eyes really that blue?"

Denise flushed, shooting color into her pasty white face. Obviously, she was not used to favorable comments on her looks. It looked to me like she was walking on happy feet to the truck. She climbed in first, then Clara and I pulled ourselves up into our seats and leaned toward the middle until the doors finally closed. It seemed like there was even less room in the cab after the Mexican food feast.

As we cruised through the northern half of Aptos toward Denise's apartment, my aunt and I were still full of chatter and giggles. Denise was quiet. Maybe she needed some solitary down time after the noisy social afternoon we had just experienced, or maybe she was having deep thoughts.

Out of nowhere, Denise said, "I think we need to set up some electronic surveillance at Eddie's place. Sheriff Sayer is pretty good at things like that." Her idea pulled me back into the real world of trying to solve the murder mystery. To me, Sayer and Lund sounded like an old married couple where each person has his or her set of job skills and responsibilities. Mom works in the kitchen, Dad takes care of the garage and back yard. If I married David, he would have the kitchen and I would be shopping for groceries and painting in the garage.

"What's on your mind, Josephine?" Clara asked.

"Just thinking about if I married David...."

"If? You don't mean that, do you, dear?"

"I didn't mean to say, 'if'...well, look who's here," I said, watching a sheriff's car being skillfully parallel parked in front of Denise's apartment building. "Not bad parking for a civil servant."

Denise laughed nervously, as my truck snuggled up against the curb right behind the sheriff's car. Calvin saw us in his mirror, climbed out of the vehicle and extended his hand to Aunt Clara as she climbed down from her seat.

"Ladies," Officer Sayer said. "Josephine, I checked the license plate number you gave me. Do you know a Rodney Plodnick?"

"The only Rodney I know is a guy who works for the Staleys. He drives a dark blue pickup...and he's a mean, nasty guy who smashed into my truck. He owes me five-hundred dollars, my share of the insurance payment."

The officer eyed my truck.

"I had some body work done on it. So what does Rod have to do with the white pickup?"

"He has title to it," Calvin said. He looked up at Denise standing on the first of four steps leading to her front door. Maybe it was the light from the fiery sunset sky or maybe she was flushed, but somehow her skin had a bit of color.

"Looks like you're feeling better," Calvin said to her.

Denise smiled slightly and nodded without enthusiasm. She marched up the last three steps, put her key in the door and slipped inside.

Aunt Clara and I looked at each other. She cocked her head. I rolled my eyes. When Sayer finally took his eyes off the door, we quickly covered our faces with blank expressions.

"What?" Sayer asked.

I looked at the dying sunset.

"What's wrong?" he asked Clara.

"I wish I knew," she shrugged. She took a couple small steps toward my truck.

"Calvin," I said, "Denise has some good ideas concerning Eddie's murder. You might want to question her," I said. "Get her mind back on work."

He looked at me with a furrowed brow and trepidation in his dark eyes.

"Just go up there and ring the doorbell," Clara commanded.

I flapped my hands toward Denise's apartment, as if to hurry him on his way.

Like a ten-year-old schoolboy, he summoned a bit of courage and dragged himself up the stairs. Clara and I scrambled into my truck and took off as the man cautiously raised his fist to knock on Denise's door.

The last remnants of a classic sunset disappeared and twinkly stars spread themselves across the dark sky. It was eight-thirty when we entered Highway One going south. Fortunately, the evening commute was history for most people.

"Oh dear," Clara said, "I think I just remembered something."

"What's wrong?" I asked.

"David called this morning before you got up. He asked me to tell you something...but I can't remember what it was."

"It's okay, we'll be home in a few minutes."

I looked to my right. Clara's head bobbed and bounced with the truck, and old lady snores competed with road noise. We rolled through Aromas where the quiet downtown section consisted of a hilly main street lined with modest 1920's and

1930's style homes engulfed in lush gardens front and back, sandwiched between a library, post office, feed store and elementary school. I turned onto Otis and parked in front of my house.

"Oh no!"

"What, Josephine?" Clara asked, shaking her head to wake up.

"Is today Friday?" I asked.

"Well, of course it is, dear...."

"I had planned to go to a Seaview Seniors meeting in Aptos." I was so mad at myself. How could I forget an important thing like that? It had been a long day, and I was exhausted and Clara looked worn out too. I checked my phone. It was dead.

"You need to charge that thing...."

"I know, Auntie. Sometimes my mind is absent, and I feel like such a fool."

"I just remembered what I forgot," Clara announced. "David asked if we were all going to Alicia's for dinner tonight." That's when we broke into tired, silly giggles. We climbed out of the truck, woke up the dogs and fed them. They acted crazy needy, wanting attention and a trip to the back yard. I checked the message machine and listened to David's sweet voice full of concern. Using the house phone, I called him and apologized for not letting him know that dinner at Alicia's had been canceled. When all that was done, Clara and I were finally able to plop down on the sofa.

"Josephine, do you think Officer Sayer is afraid of Denise?"

"Sure acts like it. And why is she so mean to him? She just turns away like they aren't even friends." I closed my eyes, relaxed and the dream began.

I was sitting between Officer Sayer and Officer Lund. Sayer was driving and Denise kept shouting directions. The car moved at a high rate of speed, backward. In the rearview mirror, I saw Rodney sitting on top of a brick wall. I saw the impending disaster and almost felt sorry for him.

Chapter 11

Saturday morning was a fresh start for me, full of good intentions. Lying in bed, I stared at the ceiling and silently vowed to do my best to make up for letting David down the night before. I would forget about murder and missing panels; and I wouldn't worry about Herbert, even though I loved that big old cat. I would keep David company all day, maybe even catch a gopher or two.

The phone rang in the kitchen. I leaped out of bed, ran down the hall and caught it on the third ring.

Clara quietly looked up from the obituaries, and David looked up from the sports page.

I picked up the receiver.

"Good morning, Jo," Alicia said. "Are you still interested in the Seaview Singles?"

I casually walked the phone into the living room. "Of course I'm interested."

"I looked them up on line to see what activities they have for their members. As it happens, they're having a beach party at Twin Lakes Beach with volleyball and a barbecue, today."

"Can you go with me?" I said, keeping my voice down.

"Sure, but are you sure you want to be away from David all afternoon?"

"We can drop in, ask a few questions and leave." Sounded simple to me.

"Come over at two," she said and hung up.

Clara and David were still reading the paper and sipping coffee. I poured a cup for myself. They were silent. I told them that Allie wanted me to help her can tomatoes in the afternoon. They nodded their heads but didn't look up from the paper. I said it wouldn't take long. They kept reading. Finally I gave up, walked down the hall and took a shower. When I came out, they were gone. Probably laughing about the cold-shoulder treatment they were giving me. I deserved it, but I didn't have to like it.

I threw on a pair of cut-off jeans and a t-shirt, gulped coffee and toast and headed over to David's orchard. Just like I thought, Aunt Clara was there, helping David bait the traps with peanut butter.

"Hi, you guys, what can I do to help?"

David pointed to the catch of the day, a brown lump lying on the ground with giant teeth and little clawy hands and feet. The critter was not breathing.

"What do you want me to do, resuscitate him?"

"Sure," David said, "and teach him how to read the 'no trespassing' sign while you're at it."

Clara laughed.

"Are you two upset because I'm going to help Alicia can some peppers?"

"What about the tomatoes?" David kept his eyes on the hole he was digging.

"We might be doing both...." I said, trying not to look at the beached rodent with the yellow buckteeth.

"Are you sure about this, dear?" Clara asked. "Tomatoes and peppers don't ripen until mid-summer."

"Actually, we're taking Solow for a run on the beach...."

"Oh, that's lovely. Can you take Sara too?"

"Ah, sure, why not?"

Solow and Sara were perfect travelers all the way to Watsonville. Sara had her head out the window, slobber flying back and sticking to the passenger seat. Solow was trapped under the dash, unable to move because of a huge Rottie in the seat that was usually his.

We arrived at Alicia's house just before two. After a brief marking session along the driveway, Solow and Sara found a fire hydrant two properties down the street, and used it for their grand finale. Alicia and Trigger helped me to load the dogs into her Volvo SUV; and we headed out of town, north on Highway One. Alicia took the Soquel Avenue exit and cruised down Seventh Avenue all the way to Twin Lakes Beach. The closest parking was six blocks away from the ocean.

Trigger helped me to put the leashes on Solow and Sara. We crossed the road, and another road and another—moving downhill with the flow of pedestrians toward a deep blue ocean full of white caps. From the street, we spotted the Seaview Singles banner flapping in the breeze, its poles knee-deep in the sand. The Singles had congregated halfway between the road and the endless waves slapping the shore. The closer we came to the Singles, the crisper the air became.

Trigger took off across the sand toward the water with Solow's leash in his clenched fist. He wore blue trunks, a gray hooded sweatshirt and flip flops. His mother wore white calf-length slacks, a sky blue tank top, sandals and a light blue sweatshirt. I wore cut-offs, a red t-shirt, sandals and a million goose bumps. Sara wore a red scarf around her thick neck. She saw people, smelled barbecue, and surged forward. I hung onto Sara's leash with white knuckles.

A dozen or so middle-aged men and women played volleyball on one side of the group's designated area, and a couple dozen older men worked the barbecues and beer station on the opposite side. In the middle, dozens of people, mostly women, sat in their collapsible canvas chairs, eating and talking.

I scanned the crowd and was surprised to see someone I knew. A large woman wearing a colorful muumuu and straw hat looked up. Bessie was way out of her drab "farmhouse in the forest" overalls. Sara began pulling me toward the woman. As we came closer, Bessie quickly folded her arms in front of her face, trying to keep Sara's sand and slobber out of her eyes and mouth.

Allie whispered, "Is she a friend of yours?"

"Yeah, kinda; that's Bessie. She's Eddie's neighbor. I've been wanting to talk to her again, so this is good." Alicia and I plopped down in the sand close to Bessie, since we hadn't brought chairs.

Sara went to the end of her six-foot leash to sniff a stranger.

"Get out of here!" demanded a large, muscular man in his late twenties, wearing a Hawaiian print shirt over his camo knee-length shorts with a gray Aussie-hat flopped over half his face. Probably color blind, I decided.

"Sorry," I said to the man, and pulled Sara closer to Bessie.

"Don't listen ta him—Brody don't know a dog from a bull," Bessie said.

"Is he with you?"

"You could say that. He's my nephew, the one I told you about." Bessie rolled her baby blues.

Trigger and Solow galloped along the shore, getting their feet wet. Just the thought of wet feet sent chills through my body.

A short stocky man wearing thick glasses, sweat pants and a "wife-beater" undershirt with stains down the front, approached Alicia.

"I can't believe that a lovely lady like you is single," he schmoosed. "If you gals need anything, just ask for Larry Bugly. Everyone knows me." He strutted away, hairy shoulders squared.

Bessie snorted, Alicia smiled politely, and I wondered how the man could have missed Alicia's wedding rings and my engagement ring. Maybe his bi-focal prescription had failed him. Or maybe everyone was automatically presumed to be single just by the fact that they were attending a singles event. As Larry walked away, sand from his feet blew in our faces. I tried hard to remember why I had loved the beach so much when I was younger. "Younger" had to be the key word.

"So Bessie, how's the neighborhood? Any strangers hanging around?" I asked.

"Pretty much nobody comes up my road." She looked away.

"Did you know that there's a homeless camp down the road?" I asked.

She nodded, like it was old news.

"So, how do you keep your house warm in the winter?" I asked.

"I have a wood stove."

Alicia looked at me funny. "Let's go see what Trigger's doing."

"You go ahead, Allie. I want to talk to Bessie." I watched Alicia stand up and plod through the sand toward the water, her hair blowing like a whirligig.

Bessie started to get up.

"Just a minute, Bessie. I wanted to ask you if Eddie had any close friends in this group."

She sighed. "The man was quiet and shy. I brought him to the singles functions just to get him out of the house, and that way I didn't have to go everywhere alone. Guess I'll bring Brody from now on. He likes the food. Is this your dog, Josephine?"

Sara had sprawled out in the sand, paws twitching, enjoying her afternoon nap.

"This is Sara. She belongs to Aunt Clara—you remember her? My dog is down there with Trigger."

Bessie turned her head to look. "It's the dog with short legs and long ears?"

I nodded. A gust of cold salty air prickled my bare arms. I shivered.

"Were there any sparks between you and Eddie?"

"I could have worked up a few sparks, but if he was ever romantic in his life—I never knew about it," Bessie grumped. She stood up and straightened her muumuu. "Excuse me, I'm gonna get some ribs." She plowed across the sand like a Sherman tank, flip flops flapping, dodging clusters of people sitting in their canvas chairs.

I left Sara snoozing and hurried after Bessie.

The men attending the row of portable barbecues looked up with welcoming eyes, swigged some beer and tried to look tempting to a fifty-year-old newcomer. They piled ribs and beans on our paper plates. I helped myself to a scoop of potato salad and followed Bessie back to her chair, back to where Sara made groaning noises in her sleep.

As I sat in the cold sand, a bearded octogenarian sitting nearby leaned closer to me. I automatically pulled my plate of food closer to my body.

"I don't want your lunch, young lady," the man said in a slow gravelly voice.

I laughed nervously. "Hi, my name is Josephine and this is Bessie...."

"I know her; it's you I'm interested in," he said, raising thick helter-skelter eyebrows.

Holding onto my plate with my right hand, I raised my left hand to brush sand off my face. Sunlight glinted off my beautiful diamond with enough glint to wake a blind man.

"Heard ya talkin' about my friend, Eddie...."

"Oh, you knew him?" I glanced up at Bessie gnawing on a rib bone, wondering why she hadn't pointed out the old gentleman.

"Twenty years ago we were in business together. I worked with plaster, stucco, cement and that sort of thing. Eddie was all about wood. He built stuff, like cabinets and he remodeled houses. 'Jack-of-all-trades,' really. We were partners," he smiled. "By the way, my name's Stucker, Fred Stucker." He held a frail, veiny hand out to me.

Letting go of the plate on my lap, I shook Fred's cold hand, which was even colder than mine.

"Was it a good partnership?"

"You bet! Eddie was a great guy if you could get him talkin'."

"A good honest partner?"

"Honest as the day is long," he grinned, revealing snowy white dentures. "And tight as a whistle with his money."

"How many years were you two partners?"

"Twelve years. Then about ten years ago I quit the business, but Eddie was still young and working hard. He was like a son to me."

"Did Eddie have a rifle?"

"Sure did. He kept an old twenty-two behind his seat in the truck. He liked to do a little bit of target practice whenever he had time, which wasn't often."

"If he was such a great guy, why would someone kill him?"

The old man tugged on his scruffy little beard for a moment. "Eddie thought that everyone was good. He never saw the bad in people."

"Are you saying that he had dealings with bad people?" I asked.

"Sometimes. Last time I saw him, about a year ago, he had rented out his basement to some fella. It was cheap rent, and Eddie complained that the guy kept taking over more and more of his space."

"Space like a bedroom?"

"Yeah, how did you know?"

"My aunt and I saw the basement full of stuff and then we saw boxes of stuff in one of the bedrooms. Who rented the basement from Eddie?"

"I asked Eddie that question a year ago, and I'll be darned if I can remember who it was."

I handed Fred one of my business cards. "Seriously, Fred, I'd like to know who's renting that space."

If I learned anything from my time at the beach, it was that if I ever went back it would be in September and I would bring along a heavy coat just in case. More importantly, I learned that Eddie had been a very decent man, tight with money and not sufficiently suspicious of people who wanted to take advantage of him. He was an easy mark.

Trigger and Solow had a great time at the beach. They tramped and splashed over the shallow slices of water left by retreating waves. Solow chased seagulls, and Trigger filled his pockets with seashells. The food was good, and most of the singles were happy to have a boy and two dogs to entertain them.

Alicia was the last to finish her lunch. She tossed her empty plate in the trashcan and announced the fact that it was four o'clock and time to leave. My heart thumped in my chest. I wouldn't be home until at least five, and David and Aunt Clara would be very disappointed in me...again.

"Okay, let's go. I have to get home in time to clean up and socialize with David and Clara. I don't even know if they have plans. No one has called me."

"I hope this trip was worth it," Alicia said, driving her car through Live Oak to Highway One.

"It was worth it. But it makes me sad to know what a nice guy Eddie was."

Twenty miles later, Alicia parked her SUV in front of her house. "Would you like to come in...?"

"Yes, but no, I can't—gotta run. Thanks for the ride, Allie."

Solow ran to my truck, leaped onto the passenger seat and claimed it for himself.

Sara had no choice but to squeeze her girth into the space under the dash. Once she was there, she could not move in any direction so she fell asleep while Solow hung his head out the window and howled every time he saw a pedestrian, a cat or a dog. I turned up the radio, and we howled and sang to the music while Sara napped. Fifteen minutes later, I drove up my driveway and cut the engine. I opened the passenger door so that the dogs could disembark in their own time.

Normally, I liked to look my best for David, but I was in a hurry to let him know that I was home. I quickly ran through my house, decided it was empty and cut across the acres of grass between my place and the Galaz house with Solow at my heels. Festive music and laughing caught my attention. The closer I came to David's house, the more raucous it sounded.

Standing on David's back yard patio, I took a moment to catch my breath. Putting my face against the glass door, I saw people dancing to an old Michael Jackson hit. Hips and arms were swinging, people were laughing, and I was frozen against the glass.

Suddenly the glass moved.

"Don't just stand there, come on in," David said, taking my sticky, sandy hand.

Solow pushed past us, scouring the floor for spilled food.

Clara walked up to me. "Glad you could make it, dear."

"I didn't know there was going to be a party..." I mumbled, as David was called away by a neighbor holding a new streamlined gopher trap.

"We didn't either. David called several friends trying to get help with this terrible gopher problem. Jimmy and his friend, Albert, showed up with some gopher bombs and a case of beer. Several neighbors showed up with traps and food. Fiona arrived later with her best friend, Mimi, and then Rico and Juan arrived."

"Why so many people?" I asked Clara.

"When David finally put out the word, everyone wanted to help. Everyone knew someone who had a gopher cure they believed in or wanted to try. The sad part is that the gophers have already made it to the new little trees."

"That's awful!" I shivered.

"Don't worry; David has another plan. Dear, you look cold...and sandy. Where's Sara?"

"At home...." at least, I hoped she was. "Let's go home and see how she's doing," I suggested. "Besides, I'd like to clean up a bit." I had visions of a three-hour hot shower.

We left Solo at the festivities and trudged across knee-deep grass to my back door.

"How was your walk on the beach, dear?"

"Cold, damp, sandy, but I have lots to tell you. I found some friends of Eddie's, and it turns out that poor Eddie was a really nice guy."

"Sara, where are you, Sara?" Clara called.

I called for Sara too as we went from room to room. Suddenly I remembered that I hadn't seen her since our ride home. I darted out the front door, straight to the open door of my truck.

Clara was right behind me.

"I'm sorry, Auntie...I was in such a hurry to let David know I was home...."

"She'll be okay. Just make the seat go back."

I tried to make the seat go back, but it only moved an inch since it was already back pretty far. Sara had pushed her way toward the door a few inches, but that was as far as she could go.

Sara's dark eyes spoke of sad confusion.

"Josephine, get David, he'll know what to do. Maybe he can lift her onto the seat."

I had never timed how long it took to get to David's through the backfields or the front route down Otis and up his driveway. Since I was already standing in my driveway, I ran down to Otis, a minute later made a right and ran up David's driveway, the equivalent of two blocks. I was out of breath when I stormed into his house.

Fiona looked at me like I was the Mad Hatter without the hat.

David came to my side looking worried. I quickly explained the problem. He darted into his garage, grabbed wrenches, screwdrivers and a crowbar and swiftly walked up Otis. Four guys followed him up the road to my place. Two of the volunteers looked very familiar. In my mind, I tried to imagine how they would look if they were unshaven and wearing work clothes.

When I finally arrived at the truck, the guys had already clustered around the passenger side, throwing out ideas on what to do next.

Clara greeted me with a hug, wiping tears from her eyes.

"Don't worry, Auntie, these guys will get her out," I said, with more confidence than I felt.

"I'm not worried, dear," she whispered. "Aren't those two young men the ones who tried to break into Eddie's basement?"

My jaw hit the gravel.

Chapter 12

Sunday morning I lay in bed making mental notes to myself, like, don't forget to go to Mom and Dad's for dinner. Next time you take Solow and Sara for a ride, put Solow under the dash and let Sara have the seat. Don't ever feed Sara beans and potato salad. Pay attention to who's feeding her, and what. Bloating is not good when a large dog is squeezed into a small space. I laughed to myself, remembering how five guys with wrenches, screwdrivers and a crowbar took my passenger seat apart. With the seat finally disassembled on the driveway, Sara stood up, shook sand from her shiny coat and leaped to the ground. Clara hugged her and cried.

The rest of the party had followed us over to my place to watch the rescue. We hauled patio furniture onto the driveway and quietly sat, watching the men who worked so hard to save poor Sara, and then we watched them re-install the passenger seat. When it was over, we dragged the furniture back to the patio, and tramped back to David's house where two other guys had meat on the grill. Looking back, it seemed miraculous how many people cared so much about Sara. Even prim and proper Fiona had carried a chair and sat with the group.

Mr. Mustache and Big Belly left the party before I could ask them a few questions, but it had become obvious that they were friends of Jimmy and Fiona.

I loved to "sleep in" on Sunday mornings. Outside my bedroom door, a vacuum cleaner roared down the hall for the second time. The motor stopped. There was a knock on the door.

"Come in, Auntie."

The door opened. Clara came in and sat on the end of my bed.

"How's Sara today?" I asked.

"Peachy keen! I was shocked to see those two men yesterday. They looked so different all cleaned up. And their wives were nice too. And I'm curious to know what you learned about Eddie…."

"Looks like we have a lot to talk about at breakfast," I said, pulling on my robe.

"I'll make an omelette with those leftover sausages from the barbecue, and the fresh eggs from Fiona. Nice of her to bring the eggs," Clara smiled.

"I had no idea Fiona was raising chickens," I said, following Clara down the hall to freshly brewed coffee in the kitchen. I tried to imagine Fiona raking up chicken poop and pulling eggs out of gunky nests with her perfectly manicured fingernails.

Solow and Sara had already positioned themselves under the kitchen table in case a piece of breakfast accidentally hit the floor. Clara puttered around in the kitchen while I showered and dressed for the day, keeping Mom and Dad in mind for the evening.

After breakfast, we decided to see what David was up to and see if he needed us to help him catch gophers. Our dogs led the way, always happy to go for a walk. Suddenly they swerved to the right and followed Fluffy up the hill behind our two houses.

"I've never seen Sara run so fast," Clara declared.

"That's because of that deranged ball of white fur ahead of them. Poor Solow, he's already way behind." I watched his head popping up over the spring grass like a bouncing periscope.

Letting the dogs have their run, Clara and I walked directly to David's orchard and found him on his knees peering into a gopher hole. We tiptoed closer, not wanting to let the rodent know how many people were after him. Not that it mattered. Three hours later, all the gophers were safe and sound in their tunnels, and David looked ready to pull his gorgeous salt and pepper hair out by the roots.

"What's the garden hose for, David?" Clara asked.

"I'm going to try something that Eddie used to do when everything else failed."

"Flood the tunnels?" she asked.

"No, I'll fumigate the tunnels," he said, with a wry smile. He turned and walked toward the garage. A couple of minutes later, he drove his Jeep into the orchard, circled around and backed up, stopping just a couple feet from a young apple tree that leaned to one side after having had its roots chomped. He turned off the ignition.

Trying to be helpful, I handed David one end of the hose. He forced that end down a gopher hole and pushed it in as far as it would go.

Aunt Clara handed the other end of the hose to David. He put on an evil smile, making us laugh, as he fed the hose into the Jeep's exhaust pipe. When he was finished, he rubbed his hands together like a fiendish killer in an old silent movie.

Clara and I stepped back from the killer hose.

David fired up the engine.

We stepped back again, keeping our eyes on the hose.

Suddenly Solow and Sara appeared on the scene, sniffing everything including the hose.

David revved the noisy Jeep.

We waved at him and pounded on his window. That didn't get his attention so we chased the dogs and tried to lure them away from the experiment, but they kept going back to the gopher hole where they started digging. Dirt flew as the Jeep roared and fumes poured into the hole.

"We need food," I shouted to Clara, "it's the only thing they understand."

She nodded, as she bent down and tried to grab Sara's collar.

I ran into David's house, opened the fridge door and pulled out two slices of bologna. "Sara, Solow," I shouted, as I ran back to the orchard, bologna flapping in the dusty air.

The hole had increased in size exponentially. Four hind legs threw clods of dirt in every direction. I dodged the clods as best I could while waving bologna, hoping to get their attention. The hole stunk like exhaust. I was desperate. Finally, I yanked the hose out of the exhaust pipe.

Clara was still shouting at David.

He finally heard or saw her and killed the engine.

All was quiet except for a disgruntled, squealing gopher that had popped out of a hole a few yards away, probably unhappy about the air pollution.

Our dogs heard the creature, backed out of the hole and raced each other to see who would get the fat little rodent first.

Mr. Gopher rolled over on his back and played "dead," so Sara had an easy time picking him up with her teeth. She carried Mr. Gopher gently over to

Clara and dropped him at her feet. It was obviously a present.

David climbed out of the Jeep, saw the gopher and said, "Well I'll be, it worked!" A moment later, the gopher rolled over and took off for the nearest hole in the ground.

"Anyone want to go to the feed store?" David asked. "It's time to get these trees into baskets."

"I'll go," I said, wanting to be with him, even if only to buy wire cages for the baby trees.

"I'll stay here," Clara said, "and take care of these crazy dogs." She already had a shovel in her hands, ready to fill in the giant hole the dogs had dug.

Fortunately, our tiny town of Aromas had a feed store that provided the best shopping around, unless you wanted something other than chicks, hay, dog food, manure, wind chimes or wire cages. We parked at the curb behind a white pickup with fancy tires and two bales of hay in the bed. The man opened his door to get in, saw us and slammed it shut. He walked over to David's Jeep, leaned down and peered into the front seats.

"Hey, Dude, great party!" he laughed, as short straight teeth peaked out from under a bushy black mustache.

"Great, except for the gophers. You remember Josephine...."

"Actually, I have not officially met your beautiful lady."

David turned to me, "Honey, this is Chris. He and Ponce worked with Eddie and sometimes they contract with Fiona."

I was stunned. What in the world were they doing for Fiona, building chicken coops?

"Nice to meet you, Mr. Mustache, I mean, Chris," I stammered.

Unconcerned about traffic, since we were in Aromas where there is no traffic, Chris leaned against the Jeep and chatted awhile. Finally, he said, "Gotta run—horses to feed and fences to fix."

"Looks like you've already fixed one fence," I laughed.

Mr. Mustache winked and nodded at me. The men shook hands and Chris walked back to his truck.

Like betrothed lovers shopping for furniture, David and I strolled the pet food aisle, the hardware aisle and rummaged through the gardening supplies. David bought ten large collapsed wire cages. He carried them out to the Jeep and stacked them in the back seat. Heading back into the hills, we found Aunt Clara still clutching the shovel, keeping watch over the various holes, ready to whack any foolish gopher that tried to surface.

"Josephine, I think Solow and Sara went home. Would you mind checking on them?" She looked at me and winked.

"No problem, Auntie," I said, watching David drop the cages on the ground near the damaged baby apple tree. I stepped closer to him. "Kind Sir, would you like to walk me home?"

It took only a moment for David to understand my true wishes. "Of course, I'll walk you home young lady," he grinned, taking my arm like a gentleman, as he steered me across a 'mine-field' of holes dug by two ambitious dogs and a million gophers. When we finally reached my back yard patio, he said, "It's been a while since we had any time alone."

Time alone was good. Solow, Sara and Fluffy roamed the property while David and I caught up on old news, new news and no news—just quiet time together, lovin' every moment until the phone rang. I looked at who was calling and reluctantly picked up the receiver because it looked official.

"Hello, Sheriff," I said.

"Ms. Stuart, I hope I didn't interrupt anything."

If he only knew! "Oh no, just taking it easy today with my fiancé."

"That's good because I'm in Aromas and want to talk to you. I'll be there in a couple of minutes." He hung up.

"The nerve!" I stamped my foot. "Deputy Sayer is on his way over."

David didn't say a word, just put his shoes on and went to the front porch while I straightened up. He chatted with the officer a few minutes, then invited him in. We congregated at the kitchen table. I made tea and brought out a plate of Clara's homemade cowboy cookies.

Sayer started off with, "I see that the door to the Garrett basement has been replaced."

David nodded, "Jimmy told me yesterday that he was going to hire someone to take care of that."

"I posted a 'no trespassing' sign on the door," Calvin smiled smugly. "We don't want anything to go in or out of that basement until we figure out if there's anything illegal going on there." Deputy Sayer bit into a cookie.

I wondered if he meant something illegal happening now, or before Eddie died, or both.

"Do you think Officer Lund will be coming back to work soon?" he asked.

"You should ask Aunt Clara. She's been spending a lot of time with Denise. Personally, I think the woman misses her work. Maybe you could encourage her to come back. And by the way, she wanted me to remind you that Eddie's place should be set up with some electronic surveillance."

Calvin raised his curly gray eyebrows as if he were considering the idea.

David put his teacup in the sink, excused himself and went home.

"Josephine, I'm at a loss. Denise gets angry every time I open my mouth."

"Aunt Clara says she's taking some new hormones, and they seem to be helping. If I were you, I'd give her one more week and then tell her someone else is taking her place. If I'm right, she won't give her spot to someone else. I think she's just about ready to get back to work."

"Well, I guess that's all...." He stood up to leave.

"One question...is anything weird going on at the Staley Mansion?"

"As far as what?" He cocked his head to one side.

"Oh, nothing, just wondered." If he could hold back information, so could I.

The back door opened and Aunt Clara entered the kitchen, huffing and catching her breath from a fast walk across the fields.

"Deputy...Sayer, David told me...you were...here. How are you?"

Sayer stood up until Clara was settled into a chair, breathing freely. He sat down again and helped himself to another cookie.

"Think you could teach Denise to make these?" he said.

"Oh my, that would be a wonderful project for us," she beamed. "Josephine, remind me to take all the ingredients and a couple cookie sheets over to Denise's apartment tomorrow."

When I was a little girl, I loved Aunt Clara's visits. She always had projects and needed my help—or so she said. It wasn't what we made so much as it was the fun we had making it. And then Mom would arrive on the scene and see the mess. Whether it was gardening, painting or baking, we usually managed to spill something, and Mom would rush to clean it up.

Deputy Sayer stood up to leave, but before he left, he handed me a key.

"What's this?"

"It's a key to Mr. Garrett's front door. I had it made so you won't be breaking in. I don't want to see you ladies in my jail—ever!" Calvin said, as he closed the front door behind him.

Clara looked at me, "I think I'll box up some of these cookies and take them to Bob and Leola's this evening. Your mother loves to make banana bread, but sometimes it misses the mark, if you know what I mean. If I remember right, Bob goes crazy over these cookies."

"You're right, Auntie. Mom never liked to bake, but her banana bread isn't bad so she uses it for all her parties. Sticks some candles in it, adds some ice cream and suddenly it's a birthday cake."

But boy could my mother dress. She was blessed with a perfect sense of style, something that Clara and I missed out on. And her parties were always fun. She knew how to make everyone feel welcome.

The afternoon hours passed quickly, as David, Clara and I worked hard to get the nine surviving little apple trees replanted inside their metal cages. It was dirty work, involving a lot of digging. The dogs looked willing to help, but they had no instinct for planting trees. They made their holes wherever they heard gophers underground, and that was everywhere.

The sun slipped down behind the hills as we patted soil around the last tree. Three showers and a bunch of clean clothes later, the three of us left Aromas in David's Jeep. I leaned left as far as my seatbelt would let me; he smelled so good, his hair still damp from his shower. We were barely out of Aromas when I noticed Clara had fallen asleep in the back seat. Next thing I knew, David was shaking my shoulder as Dad stepped out of their "thirties bungalow" on Walnut Avenue in downtown Santa Cruz. It was one in a row of six renovated homes sharing the street with doctors' offices and restaurants.

David helped Aunt Clara out of the Jeep while I hurried up the sidewalk and straight into Dad's bear hug. Mom stood in the doorway smiling. She wore a red bandage on her right thumb—same color as her red silk sari. I asked her what was wrong with her thumb. She said it was nothing much, just an excuse to wear a red bandage.

The smell of barbecue circled the house and teased us as we made our way through the living room to the little back yard where Myrtle sat, waiting for us. She stood up—her plump body looking like a blue polyester sausage balanced on spindly legs wrapped in sagging nylons. She welcomed us with hugs and all the latest news on the block since she lived right next door.

We sat around the picnic table and munched on several types of chips and dips. Myrtle crunched and talked while Dad worked the barbecue and Mom replenished various dishes.

"Josephine, dear, are you following the Eddie Garrett murder?" Myrtle asked.

"Well, kinda…." I admitted.

"I understand that you're working for the Staleys...."

I nodded. She must have heard it from Mom.

"Betty and Nibs have been friends of mine for many years," Myrtle confided. "Of course they're a bit younger, but we all enjoyed playing bingo every Thursday night at the lodge. These days we just text back and forth."

"Betty and Nibs make a cute old-fashioned couple, and I love the accent."

"I hear the Staley's cat is missing," Myrtle said, dipping a chip into salsa.

"Maybe Herbert was run over..." I conjectured, feeling pangs of sadness.

Clara's eyes widened. "Myrtle, are you suggesting that Eddie's murderer has the Staley's cat?"

"Don't be silly, of course not." Myrtle dipped another chip. Dad brought her a chili dog and all the trimmings on a paper plate.

"So, Myrtle, who do you think murdered Eddie?" I asked, piling some coleslaw onto my plate.

Myrtle coughed suddenly, her dentures clicked wildly as she coughed again and again. Finally, she was able to bring up the feisty chunk of hot dog and put it to rest in her paper napkin.

When she looked ready to speak, I again asked Myrtle who murdered Eddie. All she said was, "Cough, sputter, Village...Pub."

I looked at Clara.

She shrugged her shoulders.

The Village Pub sounded familiar to me. "Oh, I think it's a pub in Aptos." I said. "I think I've seen it when I drive through the old part of town. It's on my way to Trout Gulch Road."

Myrtle smiled and nodded her head, causing her wig to relocate a titch.

Chapter 13

First thing Monday morning, Aunt Clara and I listened to messages we had missed the night before while we were visiting Mom and Dad. The first message was from Ben. He told Clara how much he missed her, but he said he still had to go through a few more hoops to get his sister-in-law into a "home." He thought one more week would do it.

Clara put on a happy face, but I saw through it. She packed up all the necessary ingredients for making Cowboy Cookies and dropped them into a shopping bag along with two non-stick cookie sheets and a measuring cup. When that was done, she plugged in the vacuum and took it for a spin.

It wasn't until we drove through Aromas on that beautiful spring day that my aunt finally pulled out of her funk. We talked and laughed the rest of the way to Denise's apartment in Aptos. I stopped my truck at the curb, right behind Deputy Sayer's cruiser. He quickly drove away without acknowledging us.

"What's he bothering Denise about now?" Clara huffed.

"Maybe they were discussing Eddie's murder," I suggested. "Denise has all kinds of ideas...."

"Yes, she does," Clara said, "and she needs to get back in uniform."

When my aunt climbed out of the truck, I handed her the bag full of cookie-making material and her purse.

When I arrived at the Staley Mansion, Betty opened the front door, explaining that Liana was in her room upstairs with a headache and Lloyd was out of town on business.

Betty, the all-around-homemaker type, started to walk away, her black one-piece uniform looking two sizes too big on her "stick figure." Her thick gray hair was held unattractively in place with a hair net.

"Betty, can I ask you a question?"

"Of course, what is it, deary?"

"Where is Herbert?"

She shrugged, "I certainly hope he hasn't been run over or anything."

"So he is missing?"

"It would seem that way, ma'am."

On my way to the dining room mural, I stepped into the library hoping to see Chester back at work. That was a crazy thought, since everyone seemed to think he was the criminal who stole the copper panels. Just for the fun of it, I felt around for one of the two control buttons that operated the secret doors. I pushed a button and the bookshelf quietly swiveled open. Stepping inside, I noticed nine cardboard boxes stacked under the going-up-staircase. I knew immediately what was in those boxes. But how could that be? It felt like all my blood had left my body. Like a thief in the night, I backed out and closed the secret door.

I heard footsteps.

"Looking for something?" a female voice challenged.

I twirled around. "Oh, Betty, it's you...I was just looking for, ah, Herbert. Poor kitty."

"Find him, did ya?" she said with a hint of sarcasm in her voice.

"No, I'm afraid I didn't."

"By the way," she said, "your friend is in the dining room with a tall red-headed chap bedecked in jewelry and such."

"Thank you, Betty. That would be Kyle." I hurried down the hall, ready for a productive day of painting. Hopper's murky city sky was finished and waiting for us to frame each window and paint the inside walls of the Chinese restaurant. I had divided the mural into three equal sections using chalk marks. Kyle would be on the left, Alicia in the middle and me on the right.

"Like, what if my section looks different than yours?" Kyle said, as he picked through the paintbrushes.

"Good question. This is how we're going to paint this thing…we each paint the window frames and the walls in our own section, all using the same colors. Keep looking at what your neighbor's doing and try to create the same style, texture and so on. Once we get the background in, we change our routine. I will do rough placement with chalk. Allie is good at painting faces so she'll go along and create the customers sitting at the tables. Kyle, you can paint the tables and chairs, and I will bounce around putting clothes and hats on the people and food on the tables. That's roughly it, but there are lots of other things to paint, like the sign outside the window.

"Jo, do you have a print of Hopper's 'Chop Suey' painting?" Alicia asked.

"Yep, it's around here somewhere." I thumbed through a pile of computer downloads and pages torn from magazines. "Chop Suey" was hiding in the pile of ocean scenes. I taped the picture to one of the middle windows we had already painted. The idea was not to copy Hopper's painting exactly, but to recreate the same "ambiance" from the past that "Chop Suey" was famous for. I had just finished my little speech when Liana appeared in the living room, looking fine except for dark circles under her eyes.

"I've always loved that painting," she said, "I'm so glad you agreed to put it on the wall. Do you mind if I sit here in the sun and watch you?"

My first thought was, "Are you crazy? Don't you know how nervous you make us, sitting there analyzing our every move." But I didn't say that, I just smiled and said we hoped she enjoyed the sun coming in from the glass doors.

Half an hour later, Liana left her seat in the sun. The room was quiet, each painter absorbed in their new job, each of us trying to paint in the Hopperesque style which was bold and avant-garde for the nineteen twenties. Once we acquainted ourselves with the desired style of painting, things lightened up. We painted and talked and talked and painted. When I finally looked at my watch, three hours had passed.

After our first stint of non-stop painting, I toddled down the grand hallway to the powder room that happened to be located one door short of the laundry room. I heard voices: Betty's British accent and Liana's instructions. I paused in the doorway for a moment. At first the subject was laundry, then it was about Nibs quitting his job. Liana wanted him to come back to work, but Betty explained that her husband had broken out in a terrible rash caused by all the tension from working with the nasty contractor. I figured she must have been talking about Rod, because Chester wasn't there anymore. Besides, Chester had an easy-going way of running things...unless he was dealing with a dead-beat like Rod.

I heard footsteps, ducked into the bathroom and shut the door.

Two sets of feet walked up the hall, and then all was quiet.

When I got back to the mural, Kyle explained that Alicia had left to go to a dental appointment and would be back in an hour. I asked if he would like to have lunch at the nearby Mexican restaurant, and, of course, he did. The nineteen-year-old was always hungry.

Betty must have known we were leaving the house, because she stood at the front door waiting. She looked around, then leaned closer to me. "Josephine, might I go with you?" she whispered, her purse already hooked over her shoulder. The worried expression on her face told me she needed to talk.

"Sure, but it will be a bit crowded...."

"That's all right, deary," Betty said, as she scooted out the door.

Having three people in the front seat was still illegal, but at least I was dealing with a couple of very slim subjects. Betty wasn't young and agile like Kyle, but I had to ask her to sit on the console between the seats anyway because Kyle was way too tall to sit there. Even in his passenger seat, the top of his head was smooshed against the ceiling. He repeatedly straightened his glossy red crest with his fingers.

"When are you going to, like, get a bigger truck?"

"Kyle, when are you going to get something bigger than a motorcycle?"

The rest of the short ride was in silence. I parked as near to the restaurant as I could. The three of us marched in the door, and quickly occupied the last available table. Chips, salsa and menus arrived faster than fleas on a hound dog.

"Betty, is there something you want to tell me?"

"I'm afraid there is..." her voice quivered. "Me daughter works at the Animal Shelter in Santa Cruz. She called me this morning as soon as she got to work. She swears up and down that Herbert is there, at the shelter." Betty was breathless and looked ready to cry. "Nibs is in bed with the shingles, he is. Poor dear, and I can't get away. You know what Herbert looks like. Could you possibly?"

"No worries, Betty. I'll check it out right after work. Tell your daughter not to let anyone adopt Herbert before I get there."

"She's expecting you." Betty looked down at her hands. "I thought you would be the kind of person to want to help. I'll remind Angela not to let Herbert out the door no matter what."

"No worries, Betty," I smiled. "Is there a cage to put him in?"

"You'll find one in the basement room with the green door."

Finally, the woman relaxed and began eating her enchiladas and sipped her hot tea. Kyle ordered and ate like the starving young man he was, and I enjoyed a really good tostada with iced tea.

When we got back to the mansion, Alicia was already painting and Liana was sunning herself on the patio. Kyle and I took up our assigned positions and painted window frames, dark walls and splotches of sunshine hitting windowsills. Time flew. We were constantly checking the posted Hopper painting, trying to be as accurate as possible. By the end of the day, the windows and walls were finished, except for final touches (shadows and highlights).

As we were cleaning up and getting ready to leave, I asked Alicia if she would drive up to the Santa Cruz animal shelter to help determine if the cat was Herbert or not. She said she would meet me there. In the meantime, I called Denise to say that I would be a little late picking up Clara. She sniffled and said they were watching another good movie, *Hooch*.

I picked up my purse and a folded canvas tarp. Alicia and Kyle went out the front door while I headed downstairs to the green-door room to look for a cat carrier. I opened the door, and someone looked up from an oiling-something project. It was Rod. He turned red, as if I had just caught him with his pants down.

"What are you looking for?" he crabbed.

"Nothing..." I sputtered, turned around and left. I figured if I took the carrier, Rod would know something was up, and maybe he was the one who stole the cat. I didn't have time to think about it; I just left. When I got to the animal shelter, Alicia asked where the carrier was.

"Actually, I didn't bring one. Maybe I can rent one...."

"Jo, you have to have a carrier. Cats go nuts when they're in a vehicle. You'll be scratched from head to toe," she warned.

"Let's go inside. We need to look at this cat— maybe it's not Herbert." We walked into a large waiting room full of empty chairs.

A thirty-year-old woman wearing a blue smock and matching cotton pants greeted us, "Hello, is one of you Josephine?"

"I'm Josephine and this is my friend, Alicia..."

"My name is Angela. We're actually closed at five, supposed to be, but I stayed. I'll just lock this door and then we can go look at the cat." When the door was locked, she led us down a long corridor. The sound of barking and yapping dogs grew louder. I had to make myself keep walking for Herbert's sake, but I dreaded seeing dogs and kittens without homes. We turned a corner and entered another long corridor lined with dozens of large cages, each with three to five cats in them. Alicia and I looked quickly at all the cats.

"Jo, come here," Alicia said, as she knelt down for a closer look at a big, long-haired gray and white cat lying in a cage by himself.

"Oh my goodness! It's him," I exclaimed. The cat came closer and rubbed against the wire cage, his motor in high gear. He wasn't wearing a collar.

"I've only been to the Staley home once," Angela said. "I only saw Herbert once, but he's a remarkable kitty...hard to forget."

"I guess it's three out of three that think this is Herbert," Alicia said, looking a bit tired and anxious to get home to her family.

"Allie, thanks for coming," I said.

Angela walked Alicia back to the front entrance and unlocked the door for her. When she came back, I asked her if she could give Herbert a mild sedative to keep him calm in the truck.

"Sorry, I'm not allowed to do that. You don't have a cat carrier?"

I shook my head, "No."

"I hope he's the good old boy we think he is. I'm going to fudge a bit on the paper work before you go. Normally there is a process...oh well, it'll be okay. But I will need you to pay the regular adoption fee since Herbert is already in the computer," Angela muttered. "This will make Mom and Dad very happy...and the Staleys, of course. And here are a couple cans of cat food."

"Now to figure out how he got here," I said, handing over my credit card.

"Well, I'm pretty sure he didn't walk the seventeen miles from Aptos to Santa Cruz. His paws show that he's a very clean and pampered fellow," Angela said, as she held him in her arms and his motor revved up another notch. After she swiped my card, she grabbed a bath towel from a shelf of supplies on the way out, and arranged it on the passenger seat of my truck. She gently lowered Herbert into the terrycloth nest and wished me luck.

I wished me luck too. I had always admired the beauty of cats but had never owned one except for Tripod, a three-legged cat. But that was forty years ago when I was ten. As an adult, the only feline experience I had had was with Fluffy next door. I drove away with ten fingers and ten toes mentally crossed.

Next stop was Denise's apartment. I left Herbert sleeping on the seat, went up to the door and rang the bell. The girls were full of energy, having gone through two movies and five boxes of Chinese food, not that I was really counting.

"Josephine, you must be starved," Denise said. "Please help yourself to the leftover Chinese food. The Mu Shu Chicken is fabulous." Not only was this the most I'd ever heard from Denise, but she sounded so energetic and happy. Clara was a real miracle worker.

"What else have you two been up to?"

Clara put down the scissors she was using to cut out the outline of a two-foot-long shark drawn on construction paper. "As you can see, dear, we have a project. Denise has always wanted to paint fish on the big wall over there." She pointed to an eight by ten-foot space devoid of windows and doors. "It was so strange. We were watching the movie, *Three Men and a Baby* and they had murals on their apartment walls."

"Clara and I looked at each other," Denise said, "and we just knew what we had to do. I pulled out a picture of fish that I'd been saving. We're not painters like you, Josephine, but we're going to have fun painting anyway."

Denise talking about having fun—that was a first! It was almost seven o'clock and I was hungry. I helped myself to leftover Chinese and watched Clara and Denise cut out seven more fish shapes. The longest was the shark. Other types of fish were various sizes all the way down to one foot. I looked over the picture that had served as Denise's inspiration for many years. I gave her a few tips on how to paint water, lighter at the top, darker at the bottom with a shaft of sunlight streaming down through the water.

I finished my dinner and topped it off with a freshly baked cowboy cookie.

"Aunt Clara, I almost forgot, there's a cat in my truck!" I grabbed my purse.

"For a minute I thought you said you had a cat in your truck," she laughed.

"I do. Thanks for dinner, Denise, gotta run." Imagining all kinds of havoc in my truck, I held Denise's door for Clara. She understood that I was in a hurry, said a quick good bye to Denise and followed me outside to the passenger side of the truck. She peeked in the window.

"Oh my, you do have a cat in your truck. Is it bleeding?"

"No, it looks like he got hold of my red permanent marking pen."

"Boy did he! Chewed it up good!" Clara exclaimed.

"I can't take him to the Staley's with red ink all over his face."

"How am I going to get in the truck?" Clara asked.

"I'll get in my seat first and hold the cat while you get in."

"Good idea," Clara said. Moments later, she was in her seat with Herbert on her lap. "Don't you just love his soft fur and the way he purrs? Did you say he belongs to the Staleys?"

"Yep, someone stole him. Alicia and I think he might have been part of a ransom demand. Just one more problem at that house."

How does one clean permanent ink off a cat's face? I wondered. Maybe Alicia could find something about it on the internet. Or, I could wipe the cobwebs off my computer and try to find an answer. But one thing was for sure—Herbert was not going back to the Staleys until he looked presentable.

Later that night, I dreamt I was sending Herbert through a car wash. He was very brave about the sudsing and rinsing; but when the air blew him off his feet, he took off for parts unknown. I chased after him. I turned a corner at a streetlight, still on my feet running, and found Solow holding a leash attached to Herbert's collar. They stood there and smiled at me with big red lips and soap bubbles floating up from their mouths.

Chapter 14

Early Tuesday morning, I awoke with fur tickling my nose. Herbert had taken over my pillow and showed his appreciation with mega purrs. Sleep was impossible. For once, I was up before Aunt Clara. I trundled down the hall with Herbert weaving his way at my feet to the kitchen where his bowl of cat food sat on top of the fridge. With two hungry canines around, it was the only safe place. Herbert had no trouble leaping onto a chair and then up to the highest vantage point in the kitchen.

I smiled, remembering Monday night, when Herbert arrived at my house. He had received a royal welcome from Solow and Sara. They sniffed every inch of him and decided they could live peaceably together. Never mind that he looked like he had tried to apply lipstick to his lips with a vibrator. Herbert had no intention of running, so there would be no chases.

That night, David dropped in for a short visit. He just shook his head when he saw Herbert. He had no idea how to remove permanent red ink from a cat. I asked if I could borrow Fluffy's traveling cage. He said he would bring it over in the morning.

Then it was Tuesday, time to face the music. I had written down my research from the night before but had been too sleepy to follow through. The first thing on the list was rubbing alcohol. I poured some alcohol on a washcloth and rubbed Herbert's fur around his mouth. Suddenly he was not the mellow fellow he used to be. He cried and wiggled away, dragging a claw over the back of my hand as he went.

Clara clambered down the stairs from her bedroom in the loft.

"Was that Herbert crying?" she asked.

I admitted it was he, and asked her to hold the cat while I found a bandage for my hand. She sat down on a kitchen chair, and I put Herbert on her lap. His purrs were temporary. I poured hairspray on a cloth and quickly rubbed it over his face. He wasn't happy, but his reaction was mild compared to the rubbing alcohol. I poured more hairspray and gave him one last cleanup. He finally looked good enough to go home. David delivered the cat carrier in time for me to have a kiss from my fiancé, a great way to start the day!

Gravel crunched underfoot, as we sucked in the clean early morning air. Clara buckled herself into her seat. I placed the cage on her lap, circled the truck and climbed into my seat. Thirty-five minutes later, I delivered her to Denise's apartment. Clara was so excited about the fish project that she gave Mr. Kitty and me a quick goodbye and charged up to the front door. I understood her excitement. Most of my mural projects had that same effect on me.

Herbert was able to take a quick nap before we arrived at the Staley Mansion. As I drove down their driveway and parked near the house, he opened his gorgeous blue eyes wide. If he could speak, I'm sure he would have said, "I can't believe I'm home!" I carried the cage full of twenty-five pounds of cat up to the door and rang the bell.

Mr. Staley opened the door. He looked at Herbert, opened his mouth, but no words came out. A moment later, when he had gathered his wits, he leaned down closer to Herbert for a better look.

Rod stepped forward and peered out the door. His eyes were wide, but he recovered quickly.

"Is this a joke, Josephine?" Lloyd stammered.

Rod took a couple steps back into the foyer.

"You tell me. Is this Herbert?" I said, setting the heavily loaded cage on the tile floor.

"I ah, think so. I'll ask Liana." Lloyd hurried away, looking like a man who had just seen a ghost. While he was gone, Alicia drove up and parked in front of the house. She walked up the stairs and stood next to me wearing a smile.

Rod reappeared in the doorway. "Trying to make points with the boss?"

I laughed, "I don't need to make points, and I'll take that five-hundred dollars you owe me."

He quickly brushed past me and stormed out to his truck. It always felt good to see him leaving.

Liana entered the foyer. "Josephine, Lloyd was just saying...."

"Hi, Liana," I smiled.

She looked down at the cage full of gray and white cat fur. "I don't know what to say. He's not wearing a collar, but he truly looks like Herbert." She walked around the cage, studying all sides of the cat.

He meowed.

"Oh, Herbert, I missed you so much...." Liana cried.

"Now, now, my dear," Lloyd cautioned, "we need to run the tuna test before we can be sure. This is obviously a classic Ragdoll cat, but we don't know if it's Herbert."

Liana was already halfway down the hall. A couple minutes later, she came back with an open can of tuna and placed it inside the cage. Herbert sniffed the can and immediately turned his back on it.

"Oh, Lloyd, I knew it was him. Herby hates canned tuna."

"You're right, dear; he passed the test." Lloyd lifted the cage and set it down in the foyer.

Alicia and I stepped inside the house and I closed the door.

"Thank you, Josephine," Lloyd said. "We don't want Herby to sprint away, now that we finally have him back."

"But, but," Liana stuttered, "How did you find him, Josephine?"

Betty had finally arrived on the scene, standing quietly behind everyone. I didn't want to implicate her, so I said, "I happened to be at the animal shelter and saw this cat. I took him for a trial run, but if it's not Herbert I can take him back to the pound."

"Oh no, you don't have to take him back..." Liana said, as she picked up the giant fur ball, tears streaming down her cheeks.

Herbert's motor went unchecked.

I saw Betty smiling and gave her a wink.

"Josephine, may I see you in the library?" Liana asked, but didn't wait for my answer. She transferred Herbert over to Lloyd's arms, and led me down the hall to the majestic library. She sat down in an antique chair behind the massive desk, and pulled out a pen and a long checkbook. I stood in front of the desk wondering what Liana had to say.

"I can't thank you enough for bringing our dear Herbert home."

"My pleasure," I assured her.

"He's been missing since last Friday. First it was the copper panels, then Herbert. I probably shouldn't tell you this, but there was a note instructing us not to notify the police, just put cash in an envelope...you don't need to know all the particulars, but I thought I should explain some of it to you. Here is a check to cover your expenses." She smiled and handed it to me.

I thanked her for the very generous check.

"Did you pay the ransom?" I asked.

Liana nodded.

"Do you still have the note?"

Liana cocked her head as if to say, why would you want to see the note?

"Did it say they would kill the cat…?"

"Yes, how did you know?" Liana's eyes widened.

"I found a tiny piece of the note you tore up."

"And from that, you tracked down Herbert?" she asked.

"Something like that—it's a long story."

Lloyd walked into the room carrying Herbert. He looked at our somber expressions and asked me, "Has she told you everything?"

"Some of it," I said.

"You'll have to keep it to yourself. I'm sorry you became involved in this sordid business, Josephine." He put the cat down and walked out.

"Isn't he the sweetest thing?" Liana swooned as Herbert rubbed his body across my calves, over and over. "He wants you to hold him."

I picked up the twenty-pounder. Maybe he didn't eat the tuna because he was already over-fed by Aunt Clara who had offered him everything she could find in the fridge, and plenty of milk to wash it all down. When the purring started up again, I decided I could learn to love cats—at least the sweet ones like Herbert.

"Do you have any idea who took him?" I asked Liana.

"No, but it had to be someone familiar with our house. Someone who knew we were going out of town. Obviously, they had no intention of returning Herbert.

If you hadn't found him, we would never have gotten our kitty back." Liana's loving eyes rested on her cat.

"Have you talked to Chester lately?" I asked.

Liana looked to see if anyone was in the hallway. In a quiet voice she said, "Yes, we have been in contact with him. He told us that he hid the panels as soon as he discovered a ransom note someone had written. We're waiting for the Sheriff to find the people who did this. In the meantime, Chester has signed onto a construction project in Santa Cruz. We hope to have him back here soon."

"How did Chester know that someone was about to steal the panels?"

Liana laughed, "Whoever it was, tore up their first try at writing a note and dropped it somewhere in the basement. Chester said he found it, read it and immediately hid the panels. The second note was left at our doorstep the next morning. That's when they took poor Herbert instead."

Herby's purr revved at the sound of his name.

"So there was a note for the panels and one for the cat. Were they on the same yellow paper, same handwriting?"

"Yes, they were the same," she sighed. "We knew all along it was the same person. Someone with a heavy hand and poor grammar."

"What about the help? Could the perp be someone you hired?" I asked.

"Actually, your mural company and Chester and his crew are the only recent hires." She stood up. "Don't worry, Josephine, everything will be all right."

I put Herbert on the floor, and the three of us walked to the dining room together. We found Kyle and Alicia hard at work.

Liana stared at the wall, probably wondering if something that looked so bad in the beginning could eventually turn into a wonderful rendition of Hopper's famous "Chop Suey" painting. She told us how much she loved the ocean scene in the living room and kept a hopeful stiff upper lip when it came to the dining room. The 1920's Chop Suey painting was a whole new theme for us, but I was almost positive we could do it justice.

Liana went about her business, and we painters painted. A couple of hours later, I took a break, wandered down to the basement and opened the green door. From my pants pocket I pulled out the tiny piece of ransom note I had found in the library, hoping to find matching paper and ink in the basement. Absorbed in combing through shelves and drawers, I didn't hear the green door open behind me. Suddenly I knew someone was in the room. I whirled around, heart pounding, to face a familiar, mustached grin.

"Oh, Chris, it's you. You scared me."

He laughed, "You gringas scare so easy. Whatcha looking for?"

"Oh, ah, I ran out of blue masking tape," I said, as heat rose up to my face. "What are you doing here at the Staley's?"

"Ponce and I work for Rod...."

"Oh." Automatically I had a sour look, and Chris saw it.

"What's wrong with that, Josephina? We contract with lots of people, even guys who act like bullies."

"I can't imagine working for a guy like Rod," I said, pushing a drawer full of plumbing parts and pieces closed. Chris reached up to a shelf and handed me a roll of blue masking tape. "Thanks," I said. "Didn't see it up there. I'm curious, where does Rod get all that stuff he stores in Eddie's basement?"

"That I don't know—at least not for sure.," He looked around the room. Finally he took a deep breath and said, "I've heard rumors, but who can believe everything you hear?"

"So what's the rumor?"

"Maybe he orders too much, and maybe he has leftover stuff when the job ends."

"Do you really want to be a part of all that?" I asked.

Chris laughed nervously. "We just do what we're hired to do—deliver stuff, that's all. Rod lost his hammer. Have you seen a hammer anywhere?"

"Up there," I pointed to a variety of small tools hanging from hooks on the wall.

Chris grabbed a hammer and left, obviously uncomfortable with my questions. I searched the room a few minutes longer, put the blue tape back on the shelf and returned to the dining room empty-handed. We painted until one o'clock then took a lunch break. When the brushes were clean, we headed for the front door. Liana was standing there waiting for us.

"Josephine, I hope you and your friends can stay here for lunch today. Betty has made a very special feast for you. It's our thank you for bringing Herbert home."

Kyle's eyes danced at the thought of food, and Alicia and I were close behind. The kitchen table had six chairs around it and place settings for six. In the center of the table were dozens of little sandwiches covering four silver trays, everything from liverwurst with egg salad to mozzarella and tomato, even a traditional cucumber sandwich. The almond butter with spiced pear was excellent, but the best were turkey slices with cranberry and watercress. And there was not a bit of crust anywhere. I halfway expected the Queen to show up for teatime.

"I have invited Betty to join us for lunch," Liana announced, as she motioned for us to sit down. Lloyd strolled into the kitchen, pulled out a chair for Alicia and then one for me. When we were all seated, he said grace—something along the lines of, "Thank you God for this food and Herbert's safety and pardon us for eating in the kitchen." We all knew why the dining room was not an option, but Lloyd needed to make it clear to the heavens above.

I thought of this particular lunch arrangement as a giant step in evening out our various stations in life. Except that Betty had to keep getting up to serve wine, tea, coffee and slices of custard tart for dessert. However, she did manage to down a couple sandwiches and a cup of tea.

"Too bad Nibs couldn't be here," I lamented.

No one spoke.

Lloyd asked Kyle what he was studying to be. The man looked nonplussed when Kyle said he was going to become a lawyer.

My food stuck in my throat. I coughed.

Alicia looked at Kyle as if she were looking at a stranger. "Seriously, Kyle, with all your artistic talent?" she said.

He nodded. "My dad always wanted to be a lawyer."

No one spoke.

"Lloyd, darling," Liana said, "Betty's having trouble with the kitchen drain again. Is Rod around to fix it?"

No one spoke.

Finally the meal was over, and my pals and I were able to relax and go back to work. I painted a wall similar to the one in Hopper's painting, but Alicia and

Kyle had to invent their walls. In fact, everything in the middle and left side of the mural would be concocted from pictures of the right side, better known as "Chop Suey."

Late in the afternoon, Liana stopped by to inspect the painting. She stood quietly behind us until I forgot she was there.

"Josephine, Betty has gone home and I'm going upstairs. You can let yourselves out, and please lock the door as you go. And the basement door if you don't mind."

"No problem, we'll be going soon. See you tomorrow morning."

Her sturdy shoes clicked away.

Ten minutes later, we had our brushes cleaned and gear stowed. Alicia and Kyle said goodbye and headed out the front door as I rounded up my purse and sweatshirt. I almost made it to the front door, but a nagging question got the better of me. The question that kept popping up was, where do the secret stairways go? The down staircase obviously didn't connect with the basement, or the Staleys would know about it. And the up staircase—where did it go?

It was only four o'clock, so I decided to step into the library. I pushed the first button, waited for the bookcase to open and stepped inside. A pool of dim light emanated from an antique sconce. As I took a couple steps down the narrow but sturdy wooden staircase, the bookshelf closed behind me. What was the use of panicking? It was closed. I would figure it out when I came back. In the meantime, the thrill of the unknown pushed me along, step by step, as I passed under a second ring of pale light. I counted twenty-four steps, each one bringing me closer to an earthy odor. My last step landed on hard packed dirt. I stood a moment and looked around.

A four-foot-wide by eight-foot-high tunnel ahead of me featured four more sconces—four more rings of light spaced about twenty feet apart from each other. A familiar rhythmical pounding noise became louder as I walked about sixty paces to the end of the enclosure. Coming to a halt, I stood before a heavy wooden door. The source of noise had become obvious—crashing waves. I even heard the cries of a seagull. I tried turning a very old metal doorknob. It resisted at first, as if it hadn't been turned in many decades. But the knob did finally turn and I pulled the door inward, letting in a world of bright sunshine, alive with the soothing sounds of the seashore.

Stepping out the door, I turned to my right to observe some very impressive wave action in the distance. And then I heard the door behind me slam. In that same second of slow motion, I realized I was standing on a bit of crusty sand that felt crumbly under my shoes. One-second later, I rolled topsy-turvy down a thirty-foot slope, coming face to face with a very long stretch of beach and ocean.

The gulls sounded like they were laughing.

A bit stunned, I tried to stand up. That's when my purse and sweatshirt fell on top of me like an afterthought.

Chapter 15

It was hump-day, middle of the week. Before jumping out of bed to greet the new day, I snuggled under my blankets remembering Tuesday evening with my fiancé. David and I had had a lovely evening at his place, but a lot of stuff happened before I got there. I laughed to myself, remembering the Staley's steep staircase, spooky hallway and how shocked I was when the sand crumbled out from under my feet. I had rolled down the sandy hill to the beach, landing spread-eagle, limbs pointing north, south, east and west. There seemed to be no easy way back up to the house except to repeat the horrible climb that Alicia and I had endured last week after our picnic lunch on the beach.

The climb, yesterday, was just as bad as it had been the first time. Just like the first time, I was exhausted, sweaty and sandy when I finally reached the Staley's patio. The French doors were locked, of course, so I took the path that led down to the basement door because I had promised Liana that I would lock the doors before I left. I opened the back door and looked around in the dim light coming from a sconce that looked exactly like the ones in the tunnel—probably the original fixtures. Off to my right the green door was ajar. I peeked inside the room, noticing that many of the drawers and cabinet doors had been left open. It seemed odd, but I was too tired to investigate further.

Interrupting my Wednesday morning thoughts of Tuesday, a wet nose brushed my cheek.

"Solow, don't tell me you have to go out."

He licked my cheek.

I took that as, "Yes and please feed me." I slowly crawled out of bed, feeling achy to say the least. Rolling down a sand hill might sound like fun, but not when the sand is hard and there are rocks everywhere. On top of that, driftwood had been piled up at the base of the cliff, left there by winter storms. My arms and legs were scratched and bruised, but like I said, time with "Nurse David" had been worth it.

"Josephine, are you up?" Clara said from the other side of my door.

I opened it. "We're up, what's going on?" (...at seven in the morning)

"I just wanted to run the vacuum a bit—didn't want to wake you, dear."

My eyes did not roll in their sockets, but they came close. Instead, I just pulled on my robe and followed my sweet auntie down the hall to the kitchen. Clara opened the back door and Sara dragged herself inside, panting heavily after her Fluffy chase. I let Solow out the same door so that he could take up the chase. Maybe Sara had worn the cat down or at least taken the edge off of Fluffy's high and mighty attitude.

Five minutes later, Solow whined at the door to come in, his tail tucked under his body as far as it would go. He had a little pink scratch across his nose and received tons of sympathy from Auntie Clara. A piece of buttered toast helped him to feel better.

"Josephine, I'm so excited about Denise's fish project, I could hardly sleep last night."

"When I came back from David's, you were doing a great job of sleeping," I laughed, remembering her sitting on the sofa snoozing noisily. "Do you think you're going to be too tired at the end of the day to go to a pub?"

"A pub? Really?" Clara's eyes lit up like Solow's when she gave him the toast. "Haven't been to one of those since I took a trip to England with my first husband." She cocked her head to one side, squinted her eyes and gave me a half smile. "Why do I think this has something to do with Eddie?"

"Remember when Myrtle mentioned the Village Pub? I pass by the place all the time. It's just past Trout Gulch Road in Aptos."

"I'd be honored to help you out with that little chore," Clara laughed. "You know how much I love sausages."

"Are you and Denise going to paint today?"

Clara nodded and then took a sip of her coffee. "We only have three days to finish. Did I tell you that Ben called last night?"

"No...or maybe you did. I had a lot on my mind last night."

"He said he has a plane ticket for Friday. He lands at the San Jose Airport at six-forty-five." Clara put her hands over her heart and did a little twirl in the middle of the kitchen. "Ben thinks he'll be here around eight-thirty. I can't wait to see him. The parking cost for his truck will be astronomical! He had no idea it would take this long to get his sister-in-law settled, but I'm proud of him for stepping up and taking care of the situation."

"Auntie, I don't want to think about Friday. I'm going to miss you so much." I checked my watch. "I guess it's time for us to ship off to our painting jobs."

Clara grabbed her purse and twelve different colors of Nova paint in four-ounce containers, all riding in a canvas bag. Being a professional painter,

I had my preferred tools of the trade and couldn't bear the thought of Denise and Clara painting with inferior paint, which I had already seen spread out on Denise's kitchen counter. Most of the paint hadn't been opened yet, and I figured the jars might be returnable.

Clara opened the front door and shivered. We looked at each other and groaned. June Gloom had obviously started a month early. The milky fog thickened as we drove through Watsonville and became even thicker in Aptos. I drove Aunt Clara to Denise's, dropped her off and then backtracked across town to the Staley Mansion, which was also shrouded in vaporous gloom. But the soupy stuff burned off around eleven and sunlight poured through the windows into the dining room.

"Like, we should be surfing or something," Kyle said, holding his brush in the air, his head turned to face the ocean view.

"I should be weeding my garden," Alicia lamented.

"Realistically," I added, "we need to be right here, watching this painting turn into something to write home about. Has anyone seen Betty today?"

My painters shook their heads no.

I wondered if Betty had stayed home to help Nibs with his shingles. Liana was obviously trying to fill the vacuum left in Betty's absence. Her sensible shoes clicked up and down the hall many times during the day.

Finally around three o'clock, Liana and Herbert stopped by for a last look at the mural. She had changed into three-inch heels, a matching dusty-blue suit and perfume that reminded me of my favorite soap. She announced that she was meeting Lloyd in Carmel, and we should lock up the house when we left. Hopefully the lock-up would be less eventful than the day before.

So far, I had not shared my knowledge of the secret tunnel, or the movable bookcase for that matter with anyone except Aunt Clara. I was dying to tell my best friend, Alicia, that the secret button was situated on the underside of a strip of trim. Not easy to find, even after being shown. Chester obviously thought it should stay a secret, so I followed his wishes.

Around four o'clock, sunshine disappeared as thick fog moved in, blocking out the entire ocean view. Liana had already driven away in her Maserati. I gave Herbert his dinner and journeyed down to the basement to lock the back door. Alicia and Kyle cleaned brushes, folded tarps and stowed everything against the dining room wall. It was almost five when we all met at the front door.

"Like, see you tomorrow," Kyle said over his shoulder, as his long legs galloped down the front stairs.

"Jo, you look like you have plans for tonight," Alicia said.

"What makes you think that?"

"You're always so fidgety when your mind is somewhere besides the job."

"Well, Clara and I are going to have dinner at a pub...."

Alicia snorted, "I knew it; you're working on the murder, aren't you?"

"Indirectly, I guess so...."

"Indirectly, my foot!" Alicia laughed. "Just be careful and don't cause a riot."

"Yeah, Allie, you have fun too." I locked the door, headed over to my pickup and followed Alicia's SUV out of the neighborhood, happy to have taillights in front of me. It struck me as a funny coincidence that I planned to have dinner at a pub on a day that looked so damp and British.

Across town at Denise's apartment, a hint of sunlight teased me into thinking I didn't need to wear my sweater. Shivering, I rang the doorbell and waited for someone to open the door. Locks clicked and chains clanked, as Clara pulled the door open.

By the time I finished admiring the half-finished fish mural and finally collecting Clara and her purse, the fog had already invaded the neighborhood. I wanted to ask Denise to come with us; but she would have to sit between two bucket seats, risking another police stop.

"Dear, are we still going to a pub?" Clara asked.

"Yep, I wouldn't let you down, Auntie," I said, with thoughts of fish and chips and bangers and mash swirling around in my mind. Three miles and three busy traffic lights later, we were parked in front of the very classic British-looking Village Pub establishment. The parking lot was almost full—mostly pickup trucks with giant toolboxes mounted inside the truck beds. It looked like there was a contest going on as to who had the biggest tires and toolbox. Men! My truck stood out as a petite, red novelty, and I liked it that way.

Clara's chin rested on her chest.

"Auntie, we're here...."

"Oh my, so we are." She climbed out of her seat, pulled her fuzzy yellow cardigan on over her beige knit shirt, and strapped on her hippie purse. I followed her slightly teetering, just-woke-up body to the entrance door. Just as we got there, it swung open. Aunt Clara tilted backward. I caught her and held on until she was stable.

"Sorry, ma'am...oh, it's you! Remember me? Fred Stucker?"

"Of course, I remember you," I said. "This is my Aunt Clara."

Clara said, "Hello," and Fred held the door open for us.

"Did you remember who rented Eddie's basement?" I asked, as Fred backed up into the restaurant. The country-sounding Pub Rock was a bit loud, and Fred's gravely voice didn't quite get to my ears.

"Let's sit here," Clara said, as she dropped into one of four chairs circling a small round table near the entrance door.

Fred sat down in a chair between my aunt and me.

"Joan?"

"Close...it's Josephine, but you can call me Jo."

"Well, Miss Jo, as to your question, I think I remember the name...rhymes with Tod..."

"Rod?"

Fred's wily eyebrows rose up. "Yes, that's it. Don't know his last name. All I know is that Eddie didn't like him, but he didn't know how to get rid of the guy. Seems Rod was a bit of a bully."

I shook my head slowly, "I think Eddie and I were on the same page...can't stand the man! He owes me five-hundred dollars, and I bet I'll never see a cent of it."

"Maybe Rod will pay you when he gets paid," Clara said.

"I'll eat my paintbrush if that happens."

Fred laughed.

A young woman wearing all black except for a frilly white apron asked us what we would like to drink. Apparently, Fred had decided to stay a while and ordered a pale-looking ale. Clara ordered lemonade and I ordered hot tea. Clara struggled to pull off her sweater, so Fred leaned over and helped her.

The long beer bar was one-hundred-percent full and most of the tables had been taken. When the drinks came, the gal told us they had been paid for by someone in the crowd. I looked around to see if I knew anyone. Clara and Fred did the same. Our three sets of eyes all landed at the same table where Myrtle sat playing poker with three older gentlemen. She looked up for a second, adjusted her wig and smiled.

"You know Myrtle?" I asked Fred.

He smiled, "Certainly, she belongs to the Seaview Singles."

"Even though she lives in Santa Cruz?"

"We're not too particular about locations," he said, "Myrtle's the chairwoman for our annual Poker Night Extravaganza fund raiser."

I sipped my tea and thought about what Myrtle had told me. She was the reason I was sitting in the Village Pub, but I never thought that she would be there in person. But the poker part came as no surprise. The thing that really surprised me was seeing Nibs at the poker table. He saw me and instantly pulled his Giants baseball cap down over his receding hairline.

I searched the room for any other familiar faces and Clara did the same. Fred just sipped his ale and periodically wiped foam off his scruffy gray-going-white whiskers. Our waitress looked like she was in a hurry so without looking at the menu, I ordered fish and chips and Clara ordered bangers and mash. When the food arrived, Fred excused himself, saying he needed to go home. Go home to what? Obviously, the old gentleman was single. Maybe he had a cat he needed to feed.

"Auntie, do you see the man sitting next to Myrtle wearing the Giants cap?"

"Yes, I see him…" she said.

"That's Nibs—he works for the Staleys, but he hasn't come to work for a couple of days now."

"Do you know the other two gentlemen?" Clara asked.

"Actually, I think the younger guy on his right, wearing a black t-shirt, looks familiar. I think he's one of the gardeners at the Staley Mansion. I'm not sure if he's one of Rod's guys or not." I popped a fry into my mouth and groaned when it burned my tongue. My eyes wandered over to a big guy at the end of the bar wearing a yellow and green "A's" t-shirt. I recognized him as Bessie's nephew, Brody. Who could forget the shaggy brown hair?

The last two tables filled up with hungry customers. Two young couples at the table closest to us must have been new to the restaurant. Their loud conversation began with "Where are our menus?" And evolved into saying, "What's that about?" One of the girls pointed to the stained glass mural behind the bar. Her partner, a skinny guy with a shaved head, explained to her that it was a fox hunt—a sport he thought should have been outlawed two hundred years ago.

At a table further down, a tall man in his forties wearing a white t-shirt with large print on the front saying, "Pub Rock Rocks My Socks" turned to the bald guy and said, "Why don't you go pound sand, buster?" It almost sounded civil in the man's British accent. His wife, date, girlfriend, whatever, backed him up with, "You Americans know nothing about culture...."

"I know better than to hang out with broads like you," the bald guy said.

The tall British fellow stood up.

Baldy stood up to his full height—five-foot-seven, and looked up at the Brit for an uncomfortable moment, until his girlfriend grabbed his shirt tail and pulled him back into his seat.

The waitress finally arrived and handed menus to everyone at both tables. By the time their food arrived, both tables were into their third round of beer, not that I was counting. Their boisterous voices were drowning out the music. One table liked the music, the other didn't. One liked the food, the other didn't. One table accused the other of being served first. The Brit called the bald guy's tip, "meager."

Aunt Clara and I were ready to duck if things escalated. We had finished our meals and paid the bill but didn't leave because we wanted to talk to Myrtle. Finally, the people sitting at a table next to Myrtle's cleared out, and we rushed into those still warm seats. Myrtle played her last hand, counted her matchsticks, excused herself, and bopped five feet over to our table.

"Nice to see you girls," she said.

"Looks like a good night for you, Myrtle," Clara commented.

I leaned closer to Myrtle. "I've been wanting to talk to you...."

"We can talk in my car." She stood up, adjusted her wig and straightened her old-lady polyester pantsuit. We followed her outside to her car, which was not the car I remembered—the big "boat" of a car from forty years ago. Myrtle opened the doors to her shiny new, sporty red Lexus with a flick of her key. We piled in, Aunt Clara in the back seat. Myrtle's ancient little chubby body fit nicely into the driver's seat because it was pushed up and forward to the max. She turned in her seat to look at me.

"Myrtle, I know that Nibs is a friend of yours...."

"My dear, if it weren't for Nibs and Greg and Tony and Fred, I wouldn't have my new car," she chuckled. "I don't feel bad about winning, after all, they have nice retirement incomes—all I have is social security and poker."

"But Nibs isn't retired…"

"No, he isn't, but he should retire from gambling," Myrtle muttered.

"Does he gamble a lot?" Clara asked.

"Actually, he was into me for a lot of money, but he's paid up now." Myrtle patted her purse and smiled.

"How did you get him to pay up?" I asked, wondering how a little old lady could pressure a man, even a friend, to pay off his debt.

"I have a couple old friends," she smiled wickedly. "They're younger and bigger."

"How much did he pay you?"

"Forty-eight thousand dollars," Myrtle said flatly.

My jaw dropped.

"Lovely weather we're having," Clara said.

My sleep that night was fitful between dreams. I dreamt that Clara and I had adopted dozens of cats from the animal shelter and arranged them so that each cat had a gopher hole to watch. Just as we were trying to corral the last of the crazy cats, Myrtle drove up in a little clown car stuffed full of beer-guzzling men wearing Santa suits. They burst out of the tiny car, scaring away all the cats. Clara and I were so upset that we made the Santas sit and watch for gophers. David wandered by and asked if it was Christmas.

Chapter 16

Waking up Thursday morning, my mind went straight to one question—how to approach Betty about her husband's gambling. Was he really suffering with shingles? Was there a connection between Nib's debt and the ransom money the Staleys paid to get Herbert back? If not, where did he get the money to pay off Myrtle? I thought about Herbert and the copper panels while I showered. Were the panels originally meant to be the answer to Nib's debt? I sipped coffee and ate burnt toast, too busy thinking to taste anything.

There were a few drawbacks having Aunt Clara as a houseguest. Her natural enthusiasm drove her to vacuum the house, pull weeds and cook. Her coffee was bitter, the toast always burnt and those were the best items on her limited menu. But I would miss her like crazy when it was time for her to leave.

"Good morning, dear," Clara said, refilling my coffee mug.

"Oh, sorry Auntie, my mind was on…."

"Myrtle and Nibs?"

"Yeah, and it doesn't add up to anything good."

Clara shook her head slowly, "Unless Nibs won the lottery."

"Have you heard any more from Ben?" I asked.

"Just a short message last night saying he's still set to come home Friday. I'm so excited. I must sound like a new bride…" Her cheeks were extra pink and her fluffy hair bounced with a turn of her head.

"You are a new bride, Auntie. It hasn't even been a year—and look at you blush. I'm so happy for you."

She looked at my beautiful engagement ring and said she was happy for me as well. I still wasn't quite used to the idea of getting married again someday. But on the other hand, I couldn't imagine myself without David in my life.

Motoring north, across the southern half of Santa Cruz County, my aunt and I were unusually silent. As we entered Denise's Cabrillo College neighborhood, Clara asked if I would like to come in and see the fish mural, and critique it.

"I thought you'd never ask," I laughed, as we clamored out of my pickup and up three steps to Denise's front door. She opened it before I had time to ring the bell. Her smile was starting to look like a natural feature. Dressed in grungy old paint clothes, her pale blue eyes sparkled. Obviously, Clara had poured a lot of new life back into her empty shell.

Denise ushered us in and proudly stood beside the eight-foot by ten-foot light blue wall that darkened near the floor as colorful fish swam deeper into the ocean. She explained that she and Clara planned to add a sandy bottom to the picture with rocks, seaweed and a few critters like crabs and maybe an octopus. Even without the sand, the wall made me feel like I was standing outside a giant window looking in at all the beautiful fish in the ocean.

"How about a chest full of jewels and treasure?" I suggested.

Clara and Denise gave each other thoughtful nods. Neither of them liked to wear jewelry, but they liked the idea of a trunk full of bling, as long as it was under water.

They didn't need me to critique the painting. It was lovely and peaceful just as it was. I felt proud and happy for both of them, because I knew that wonderful feeling of excitement and satisfaction when a project was almost complete.

Before leaving the Cabrillo neighborhood, I called Alicia and asked her if she would like to go to lunch at the Village Pub. I hadn't told her that Clara and I had already been there once. There would be plenty of time to talk about it while we painted. I would tell her how good the food was, but I really wanted to see if Myrtle would be there again. Did she have a gambling addiction? I worried about her all the way to the Staley Mansion. By the time I parked the truck, I had finally talked myself out of worrying about Myrtle. At eighty-years-old, she was old enough to know what she was doing. She would keep winning and would be all right, I told myself.

Spring semester at UCSC was over, and Kyle arrived on the job in good spirits. Alicia parked behind his yellow Honda motorcycle. We were greeted at the front door by Liana, who looked about three blocks short of her usual perfection. A few red hairs were loose and she wore mismatched earrings.

Herbert leaned against Liana's ankles, purring his heart out.

Liana ushered us in, quickly scuttled down the hall and disappeared into the kitchen. From the dining room, we heard pots and dishes clunking in the sink as she loaded the dishwasher. Obviously, Betty was still absent.

We painters stood for a few minutes in front of the Chop Suey painting discussing areas that worked well and ones that weren't quite up to speed yet. The perspective was right on, but there was something wrong with the lighting. We were dealing with a hazy day outside the restaurant windows, and electric light coming from fixtures inside the establishment. Mr. Hopper had created a classic painting with the use of strong color, deep shadows and splashes of brilliant light. A tall order, but we were determined to get it right.

Mid-morning, I asked Kyle if he wanted to join Alicia and me for lunch at the Village Pub. As far as I knew, Kyle had never ever turned down food, and his lanky body never gained weight. As predicted, he was happy as a puppy to be going to a new place to eat.

"I'm sure our lunch has something to do with solving a mystery—but I'll play along and hopefully enjoy the food," Alicia said. "Don't look at me like that, Jo, I'm no food snob. I like all kinds of food," she said, as she painted in a patch of sunlight.

Half an hour before our lunch break, I dropped my paintbrush in the water jar, strolled down the hall, listened at the library door, entered and quietly closed the door behind me. I figured Liana and Lloyd were upstairs working in their office. It was time to try the second secret staircase—the one that went up. I ran my fingers along the wood molding, found the right button and pushed it. The bookcase silently swung open. I entered a small room lit by one sconce, possibly connected to a motion sensor or some other automatic device. Four boxes of copper panels were stacked under the staircase.

Trying to be extra quiet, I kicked off my running shoes and climbed the stairs in my socks. I counted seventeen steps to the top, and the top was a nothing little platform with walls on three sides. On my left about five and a half feet up the wall, basically eye-level, was a thin round piece of metal about four inches in diameter. I felt a small metal handle connected to the right side of the circle. I pushed it, and finally pulled it toward myself. The metal piece swung open, revealing a fine metal screen. From where I stood, it looked like the screen was covering a hole in the wall behind a large piece of furniture, possibly an armoire. Through the device, I heard someone sneeze.

"Bless you, dear," Liana said.

"Thank you, my pet," Lloyd answered. "By the bye, how is the dining room painting coming along?"

"Actually, I've been so busy doing Betty's work, I haven't taken the time to check. Maybe I should do that now...."

Immediately I scurried down the stairs and pulled on my shoes. I hurried into the library and hit the button to close the bookcase.

Footsteps clicked down the hall.

I opened the door and stepped out into the hallway.

"Josephine, were you looking for me?"

"Ah, actually I was...I wanted to show you the progress we made today."

"Lovely, let's take a look," and off we went.

Alicia and Kyle had already cleaned the brushes and stacked the paint against the wall.

Liana backed up against the opposite wall of windows, her back to the Pacific Ocean. Her gray-green eyes were exclusively trained on the painting, as she pursed her lips and blew out a little air.

"I'm beginning to see what this is going to look like...and feel like. It's very intense, isn't it?" she exclaimed, "Also friendly and comforting."

Alicia stepped closer to Liana and observed the painting. "I wonder if those days were as colorful and romantic as Hopper depicted them?"

"Let's face it," Kyle said, "life, artwork means different things to different generations."

"Very astute, Kyle," I said. "What does it mean to you?"

"It reminds me that I'm hungry."

Alicia chuckled, and Liana's face lit up in a big smile.

Herbert wandered into the room. "Herbert, darling, do you like the painting as much as I do?" Liana asked, picking up the overweight kitty. Herbert answered with a full-throttle purr.

Soon after that, Alicia drove Kyle and me over to the Village Pub in her SUV. We entered the restaurant. At first, the lunchers were pretty quiet compared to the night customers. I didn't recognize a single soul, except the waitress, who wore the same all-black outfit with the lacy white apron and her black hair in a long straight ponytail, with bangs covering her forehead down to her eyelashes. She gave us three menus and three waters.

"Looks very British," Alicia commented, staring at a red phone booth with windows, stationed in the corner of the room behind our table.

Kyle nodded. "Just like the old movies."

Suddenly the entrance door burst open and half a dozen construction workers poured into the room, making their way to the bar. Obviously, they were regulars. Their meals arrived before ours and the beers on tap just kept coming. One of the guys was Rod. I also recognized Chris, Ponce and Brody. Their bill came and Rod told the waitress to charge it to his account. She said she couldn't. The boss told her no more charging.

I watched as Chris pulled out a credit card and paid the bill.

So, Rod was short on money. He worked for the Staleys; why was he hurting for money? *Maybe he played poker with Myrtle,* I laughed to myself.

"What's that silly grin about?" Alicia asked, and popped a French fry into her mouth. "These fries are really good."

"They're like the best I've ever had," Kyle said. "I like the fish too."

"Jo, has Rod paid you the five-hundred dollars he owes you?" Alicia asked.

Kyle's mouth dropped open. "You mean the guy over there owes you money?" Kyle said, looking at me.

"Yeah, before you started work at the Staley's, Rod ran into my truck. Now it looks like I'll have to wait for the money—maybe forever."

Minutes after the workers left, Myrtle and Fred entered the building.

I stood up and walked over to their table. After warm greetings, I sat for a few minutes and chatted with them.

Myrtle yawned, "Oh my, late getting home last night, weren't we Freddy."

He nodded and tried to stifle his own yawn. "We'll go home earlier tonight, won't we, dear?"

Oh my God! Myrtle had a boyfriend. I tried to be calm, but I liked Fred and felt so happy for her. But they were so old. How could such a thing happen? I checked Myrtle's chubby little hands for any new rings, while we chit chatted about my folks. But I didn't see a ring. She told me that my mom had her car in the shop, and maybe I should go see her. That made no sense at all, but I made a mental note to call Mom at my first opportunity. Mental notes were slippery little critters that sometimes escaped into the ether if I didn't write them down.

"How's your sister, Myrtle?" I asked.

"Who? Oh, she's fine…"

"It was great to see you two," I said to Myrtle and Fred as I stood up to leave.

We said our goodbyes.

I caught up to Alicia and Kyle who waited for me at the door. Kyle held it open for us.

"Sorry, Allie," I said, as Kyle let the door close behind us. "I was going to pay...."

"Kyle paid," she said, looking like proud mothers look when their sons act like gentlemen.

"Thank you, Kyle."

"It's okay, tomorrow's payday," he grinned, which reminded me that Friday was just hours away. I didn't want to think about what would be my last day with Aunt Clara for a while.

Alicia pulled her car into traffic and soon we were back to work on the mural. As usual, I put painting on autopilot and ran various ideas through my head. Was the basement passageway originally for bootleggers in the twenties? Had Chester explored the tunnel? Had Nibs learned his lesson about gambling? Why did people do stupid things?

"Jo...Jo to earth," Alicia said.

"Yeah, what's up?"

"How many people should I put at this table? So far it looks like the whole wall has tables-for-two."

"Sure looks like it. Let's stick to one or two at a table. We don't need to be painting whole families and small conventions," I said.

"Like, don't we need a waiter somewhere?" Kyle asked.

"I think a waiter in your section would work well."

Kyle laughed. "I knew you were going to give it to me. What does this waiter look like?"

"Chinese, and male, of course," Alicia said, "black hair, black slacks, white shirt and a vest."

"Thanks, Allie; like, I can picture that," Kyle said, already sketching in the waiter carrying a tray at shoulder height.

Since my section of the mural was eighty percent done, I decided to take in a bit of sea breeze before getting back to work.

After twenty minutes of sun, salty air and a swift breeze, I felt refreshed and went back to Chop Suey. As I painted a steaming teapot casting a deep purple shadow onto a white tablecloth, I thought about a new project Liana had recently mentioned. She wanted us to paint fish on a three-foot high by thirty-foot long concrete garden wall that curled in and out, bordering a section of colorful succulents growing beyond the back patio. There were two possible difficulties—the weather and the fact that there were only eighteen inches (after the plants had been trimmed) of sidewalk to stand on while we worked. Kyle's feet would need the whole space. The concrete wall was the last structure before the property began its downward slope, covered in regional ground cover plants, ending in a steep cliff that eroded a little bit every winter when the high tides and wild rain storms attacked it.

"Allie, what do you think about painting the wall with fish?"

"I like the idea," she said, dipping her brush into a dollop of burgundy and mixing that with a spec of mars black. "I think the fish should look like jewels or stained glass—pure bright color against a deep blue sea."

"Like, I can see that," Kyle said.

"I can too," I said. "I'll order a gallon of cobalt blue for the background. But the first coat of paint will be a primer. I'll pick up the primer over the weekend because I think this Chop Suey picture will be finished very soon. Your waiter is looking fantastic, Kyle."

"Thanks, I modeled him after a guy that works at 'China Gardens.'"

Working down from the ceiling, we were finally finishing up the three-foot space above the wainscot. That was where the tables and people were located. What a relief it was to not be standing on ladders. Our next mural job would not require ladders at all, just lots of bending and squatting.

"I'm going to take the six-foot ladder back to the basement since we won't be needing it any time soon." I collapsed it, tucked it under my left arm and proceeded down the hall. As I clunked down the stairs to the basement, I caught a flash of someone at ground level darting out the back door. The green door had been left wide open. I entered the room and leaned the ladder against an empty wall. A quick look around told me that the room looked different—emptier somehow. I wondered if Rod darting out the back door carrying a large sack of something had anything to do with the emptiness.

I thought about the green-door room as I drove across town to pick up Aunt Clara. Once I had made a mental inventory of the tools that were usually stored on the walls and in cupboards and drawers, I made a mental search for those tools in my recent memory of the place. I worked at this puzzle so hard, I almost missed the turn for Denise's neighborhood. Making a last-minute right turn, a horn honked. A sleek convertible passed me, barely missing an oncoming car. Johnny Law happened to be sitting on his motorcycle in the shade of a large pine tree. Mr. Convertible had words with the cop while I cruised two more blocks to Denise's place.

Just as I pulled to a stop at the curb, my cell phone rang. I quickly dug into my purse and answered. "Fiona? What's wrong?"

"An associate of mine just told me that Eddie's house burned down today. I thought you might want to check out what happened since you're working in the Aptos area."

"Yeah, I will…what happened? How did it catch fire?"

"All I know is what I just told you," she said, and hung up.

She didn't sound very upset. I didn't know what to believe, but I would certainly check it out.

Aunt Clara opened the door for me.

"Something wrong, dear?" she asked.

"I'm not sure. Let me have a quick look at the mural and then we'll be on our way." I stepped inside and admired the painting. The soothing underwater scene almost washed away my worries about Eddie's house, but not quite. The ladies had added a "bottom of the sea" with sand, rocks and all sorts of critters. There were several crabs, one of them a small hermit crab living in a vacated muscle shell.

"Hi, Denise, this is amazing. How did you paint so close to the floor?"

She laughed, "We were lying on the tarp. Isn't that how you do it, Josephine?"

"I usually sit curled into a ball while I paint. I call it the "impossible paint pose." There's no easy way to paint that bottom area and getting up is the worst!"

"Is something wrong, Josephine?" Denise asked.

"Maybe…not sure yet. I think I need to check out Eddie's property." My stomach lurched, which was usually a signal that all was not well.

Chapter 17

Aunt Clara and I had no idea Denise would want to follow us in her car, but there she was right behind us as we pulled into Eddie's driveway. Even before we climbed out of the truck, Clara said she smelled smoke. Denise came to my window and said she smelled smoke. I looked around and saw smoke coming up from Eddie's chimney. What a surprise to find the house intact and a friendly fire in the fireplace.

"I wonder why there's smoke coming out of the chimney," Denise said, "when no one lives here and there aren't any cars other than Eddie's truck? Judging by the color of the smoke, I believe it's oak—a bit on the wet side."

"I wonder where Fiona got her information?" I said, feeling like someone wasn't being honest. But why would anyone tell Fiona that Eddie's house had burned down? "Look at these tire prints. Looks like someone parked down there, near the path to the basement."

Denise walked down the gentle slope and stood where the tire tracks ended. "Looks like a large U-Drive truck, heavily loaded, was stuck in the dirt—really dug a deep hole here trying to get back up the hill," she said, as she examined every inch of the tracks, then bent down and picked up something shiny.

I looked around and found more shiny nails.

Clara was already heading down the path to the basement.

I was curious too.

Denise decided to tag along and find the source of the nails. "This is interesting." She pointed to a newly installed metal basement door embellished with a couple of heavy chains and a heavy-duty padlock.

"Looks like Jimmy's trying to keep people out," I said.

"If that's the case, why isn't the door locked?" Clara said, pointing to the unengaged chains and locks. She turned the doorknob and pushed on the door. It opened. She stepped inside and felt around for the light switch. Fluorescent lights flickered on.

We gasped. To our great shock and surprise, the basement was not the way we had left it, full to the brim with hardware, tools and siding. The large room had been stripped of everything of value. All that were left were empty beer cans and empty Cheetos bags. One bag moved. A mouse crawled out of the bag, raced across the room and hid under the stairs.

I shivered. The room was cold and mice lived there!

Clara huffed and puffed up the stairs only to find the kitchen door locked. She turned to come back down.

"Careful, Auntie, that step doesn't look right..." I shouted.

Denise and I could see that the step wasn't right—it was loose and not resting on the frame squarely.

Denise moved up three steps for a closer look.

"The step is loose...!" she warned Clara.

Clara already had one foot in motion. It hit the step, the wood flipped into the air and she went sailing into Denise, who tumbled backward all the way down to the concrete floor. Clara landed on top of Denise.

In that same terrible second of slow motion, the top step flew sideways, landing on the floor close to where the mouse had disappeared. The mouse shot out from under the staircase in full panic mode and ran up my leg.

"Why are you screaming, Josephine?" Denise asked in disgust. "It's Clara and I who should be screaming."

"The mouse! The mouse! Get him off me!"

"He's off, and he's more scared than you are," Denise said, as she tried to help Aunt Clara stand up.

I tried to help steady Clara as she tilted badly to one side.

"Denise, let her sit." We helped Clara plop down on the second step with a whimper.

The metal basement door suddenly slammed shut.

We whirled around and listened, wide-eyed, as chains clanked.

"What was that?" Clara groaned.

Since I was the only one standing, I turned and charged the door with my whole body. I turned the knob and pushed hard on the cold metal. I heard the click of a padlock closing.

"That's what those chains were for," Denise said, her voice like cold steel.

I pounded my fists on the door, seething, "If I ever see Fiona again, I'll drive my truck straight into her fancy Lamborghini…"

"I'd punch her right in the nose," Clara said.

"I'd shoot her," Denise said. "Is she supposed to be a friend of yours?"

"Not really a friend," I said, "but I was trying to like her for David's sake."

"Did you hear that?" Clara whispered, pointing to the ceiling, which was primarily the kitchen floor.

"Yeah, footsteps," Denise said, "hundred and eighty pounds, size 11 shoe."

Clara and I looked at each other.

"Just kidding," Denise laughed. "It's actually a little old lady wearing rubber boots."

"How do you know that?" Clara asked.

"I don't know who's up there, but I did hear footsteps." Denise shrugged her shoulders. "Ouch, my hip feels like it landed on concrete."

"It did," Clara said with a straight face. She looked at Denise and realized the cop was just trying to be humorous. Even though my poor aunt had suffered a twisted ankle, she suddenly broke into a fit of laughter. Laughter was the best thing for breaking the tension we all felt. As captives, we couldn't do much, but we could laugh.

"If tough guys open the door and come down the stairs, all laughing should be canceled," I said. "Unless they don't notice the step is gone and fall through it, then we can have a great laugh." The laughing continued.

"What about the guy behind him?" Denise asked. "What if he trips over the first guy, rolls down the stairs and lands on top of us?"

By that time, we were howling with laughter. Good thing, because in reality there was a lot to fear, and more to come.

"I think we should knock on the kitchen door..." Clara suggested.

"I don't think the old lady wearing rubber boots will accommodate us," I said.

Another round of laughter.

"Sure is chilly in here," Clara complained, as Denise pulled her up to a shaky standing position. "Thank you, Denise, but I think I'll just sit here on the step."

Denise eased her back down. "Josephine, what time is it?"

"It's six-thirty, and you can call me, Jo." My stomach gave a little gurgle, which it always did around dinnertime. The one comfort we had was light. The lights were still on and would stay on because the fuse box was mounted on the wall next to the stairs. We discussed pulling all the fuses out except the one for the basement, but Denise thought that would be like swatting at a bee's nest. Somehow that triggered another round of laughter. It was either laugh or cry and we chose the former, at least up to that point.

"I think I heard a door close upstairs," Denise said.

We waited in absolute silence for any other sounds, like someone coming to the basement door or the rattling of chains. But that didn't happen.

"That was the hundred and eighty pound guy leaving the house in his 1998 muscle car with yellow flames painted on the sides," I said.

No one laughed. Nothing was funny anymore. Reality had caught up to us—its cold gray truth crept into our bones. We had had no plans to stay at Eddie's place very long and since no one else was around, we never gave a thought about leaving our purses unattended in the vehicles. Denise, being on leave, was wearing her civilian clothes, paint clothes actually. There was no belt with five types of weapons attached to it. All she had was a phone in her pocket, and it was out of juice.

My mind was in a whirl—so many thoughts, so little time. Since Eddie's truck was the only vehicle on the property, was someone using it? Obviously, someone had set up the place to look quiet and inviting. But there was some cold calculating going on, like waiting for a mouse to walk into a trap. And then I realized that the trap had already snapped.

Denise finished studying the situation first and broke the silence.

"There are no windows, only two locked doors. We can't budge the chained door so I think we need to try to open the kitchen door."

"But how?" Clara asked.

"Let's look for any kind of sawing or cutting tool," I said, as I walked over to a long workbench against the wall. It had three shallow drawers built into it, and all three were empty. Someone had done a very complete job of emptying the room. But why?

"I smell the fire in the fireplace...." Clara remarked.

"Might not be the fireplace," Denise said.

All of a sudden every cell in my body froze. I knew why someone had emptied the basement and lured us into it. And why someone told Fiona the place had burned down. That person thought I was getting close to the truth and wanted to get rid of me, and poor Aunt Clara and Denise would be my collateral damage.

Chapter 18

Eddie's basement ceiling, slash kitchen floor, was going gray. Not a pretty gray, but a smelly gray and the smoky smell had Clara, Denise and me covering our mouths with our shirts. My eyes stung and my heart pounded in fear. Both doors were impossible to open, and no one even knew we were missing. We sat on the cold concrete floor and prayed for help to come.

The mouse didn't seem to know that his life was in danger. He skittered over to an empty bag of chips and crawled inside. Maybe that was the smart thing to do. I left the mouse alone but gathered up three other mostly empty Doritos and Cheetos individual-size bags. I gave one to Clara and one to Denise. Just the smell of the chips made my stomach feel cheated, as I ripped two sides of my bag open and held the crunchy plastic over my mouth. The three of us had a few good Cheetos-flavored breaths.

Aunt Clara coughed.

My heart sank. "I'm so sorry, Auntie." My throat stung when I spoke.

"It's not your fault, dear. Next time I see Fiona, I'll pull her hair right out."

"And I'll back up my truck and hit her car again," I groaned.

Denise was quietly saving her breath, but her pale complexion had gone pure white. The upper half of the room had literally disappeared into the smog, and Mr. Mouse had tucked himself away under the stairs. As much as I hated mice, he was probably going to be the last animal I would ever see. I bent down and crawled under the stairs. The mouse was nowhere to be seen, but his hole-in-the-wall home was right in front of me. He had chewed a hole in the wallboard. I noticed that a tiny bit of fresh air whistled in from the hole.

Clara and Denise looked like they were about to fall asleep—the kind you don't wake up from. I scrambled back under the steps and began ripping wallboard with my bare hands. Dang! There goes my nail. No time to worry about that, I reminded myself, as I tore away small chunks of unfinished wallboard. Like a rat, I was making the rat hole bigger. The incoming air was musty, like the dirt smell in the secret tunnel at Staley's Mansion, but quite refreshing compared to the smoky basement.

It was time to share the air. "Denise, Clara, come over here and get some fresh air." I tugged on my aunt's arm, trying to get her to stand up. Denise was already heading for the rat hole.

"What did you just tell me, dear?"

"We need to get some fresh air. Follow me."

A few tipsy steps later, we were looking at Denise's backside as she got down on her knees, stuck her face in the hole and breathed deeply. Clara took a turn sucking air and seemed to be more alert for the effort. The three of us took turns ripping wallboard and sucking air, as we wriggled in and out of a space smaller than the cab of my truck. The hole grew slowly but surely until it was big enough for a basketball to passed through it.

"Do you hear a crackling sound?" Aunt Clara asked us.

Denise and I looked at each other, not wanting to talk about what was actually happening. Obviously,

Clara wasn't a hundred percent aware of how bad our situation was. We didn't want to upset her but she needed to know, so I explained to her that the house was burning down, but we might be able to squeeze out the rat hole if we worked hard and enlarged it fast enough. The widest we could make the hole was eighteen inches because of the vertical studs, but we could go up three feet before we would be stopped by a cross beam.

"We have six minutes tops to get out," Denise said, in her 'official deputy-sheriff tone.'

"It'll be okay, Auntie," I said, "we'll be out soon." Perspiration ran down my unnerved, unconvinced, lying face.

Denise tore into the wall with all her might, she being at least ten years younger than I. The bigger the hole got, the more fresh air we were able to breathe. Clara and I were right behind Denise, cheering her on. Behind us, the room was disappearing from view. Our eyes smarted. The once distant crackle and roar became louder. My heart pounded.

"Looks like we have an outer wall in our way," Denise informed us.

"Okay, Denise, let me give it a go," I said. "We'll worry about the next layer when we get there."

She backed out and I tore into the project with every ounce of strength I could muster and never mind all the broken fingernails. The rat hole grew, looking like a large open mouth with lipstick. *The lipstick was our red blood, but skin heals,* I kept telling myself. A couple more minutes and I gave it up to Denise. With renewed energy, she was able to finish that layer. She then turned over onto her back and jabbed her legs through the hole, her feet hitting the outer wall hard.

"Do you hear sirens?" I said, my hopes rising.

"Yes dear, but how will they find us?" Clara asked between coughs.

"We'll be out soon, don't worry," I said, as Denise slammed the exterior siding over and over with her feet. I heard the wood crack. She hit it again. It cracked again. She was breathing hard between coughing fits.

"Denise, let me take a turn," I said, sweating buckets of perspiration.

She scooted out from under the stairs and I took her place. Slamming wood with my legs and feet was not as easy as I thought it would be. Three slams and my legs complained. But I felt the wood give—just a bit. I slammed it two more times. The wood cracked. Straight ahead, I saw giant boots through the splintered wood.

Denise reported that the kitchen door was on fire.

Someone pulled on the siding from outside. The resisting outer wall screeched, as nails bent and ultimately gave up their hold. Finally, we saw a clear path to safety.

The fire had spread from the kitchen door to the top steps.

"We need to get out ASAP!" I coughed, "Denise, you go first, then Clara and I'll go last."

Denise's long skinny body dove through the hole head first. Someone outside held the siding back and then helped her to her feet.

"Quickly, Auntie!" I gave her a nudge.

Two large gloved hands reached in and took hold of Clara's arms. I pushed from behind. It was tight, but she wriggled through. I followed close behind and flopped on the ground to catch my breath.

A fireman helped me up and walked me over to one of the fire trucks parked in the driveway. Denise and

Clara were already sitting in the front seat when I got there. We sat side-by-side, passing oxygen back and forth, each of us taking two gulps at a time. The fireman left us to go help his pals fight the fire. We had a front row view, and it didn't look like anything would be saved. Keeping the trees from catching fire was of utmost importance. There were enough trees to set off a giant forest fire.

After a while, a young fireman checked on us, asking if we needed medical help or the hospital perhaps. We told him we were fine and glad to be alive. He helped us out of the fire truck and over to our vehicles. We gave him our phone numbers and promised we would help with investigations of the incident. Thankfully, we were allowed to leave.

Denise and Clara hugged.

As Denise walked to her car, a man wearing Levis and a white t-shirt came up to her. We watched as they embraced. He opened the car door for her.

"Isn't that man...?" Clara uttered.

"Yeah, it's Calvin. I almost didn't recognize him, looking sharp in his off-duty clothes," I said, and checked my watch. It was only a little after eight, but it seemed like we had been trapped in Eddie's basement for hours and hours—days, actually.

Calvin skillfully backed Denise's car out of the driveway, avoiding two fire trucks and his own vehicle. I backed up my truck following his lead. When we were finally back to the road, I gave a sigh of relief.

"Are you all right, dear?"

"I was going to ask you the same question, Auntie."

We waved goodbye to Calvin as he turned and walked back to his late-model sporty car. Suddenly we were giggling, the tension having dissipated and finally we were heading home.

One of my dreams that night included a handsome fireman who looked exactly like John Wayne. He pulled off his boots, and I recognized his feet. It was David. When we kissed, he smelled like burnt barbecued ribs.

Chapter 19

At breakfast, I asked Clara if she would like to
stay home and rest after our traumatizing ordeal the
day before.

She shook her head, no.

Thursday night we had long hot showers, but
Friday morning my aunt and I still had a hint of
smoke about us. Solow and Sara must have thought
we brought home barbecue take-out of some sort and
kept sniffing our shoes.

"I feel charged up and ready to go finish the fish
painting," Clara said.

"Seriously?" I took another bite of toast.

"Sure, my body needs to keep moving or I'll
turn to stone. My mother—your grandmother—used
to tell us that whenever Leola and I lolled around too
much. Actually, it was I lolling more than your
mother. Leola was the one with all the friends and
places to go."

"Auntie, that's why you and I are so much alike.
Now, are we going to tell the men what happened
yesterday?"

"You mean before they see it on TV?" she
laughed, and sipped her coffee.

"You mean…?"

"Dear, the KAPUT crew left just before we did.
Didn't you see their van with all those funny little
antennas on the roof parked on the side of the road?
We followed the van into Aptos."

"Sounds like you were less traumatized than I was." I sipped my coffee, trying to remember details other than my panicked state of mind and how much my fingers hurt. I looked at my stiff, sore fingers. The skin didn't look nearly as bad as the fingers felt on the inside—just torn fingernails, small cuts and scrapes. Like Aunt Clara, I felt I should keep my hands busy so they wouldn't stiffen.

"I'm so glad the forest didn't catch fire," Clara sighed, looking at the bright side as usual.

Taking another look at my raw, ravaged fingers, I decided I was lucky to be alive. "If Eddie's a ghost, I wonder how he feels. After all, he lived in that house most of his life."

"Ghosts don't cry, my dear."

"Oh, and you know all about ghosts?" I teased.

"Well, at my age, I'm practically there," she laughed.

"Remember, you're as young as you act—so that makes you about thirty-five-years old." We laughed until our sides hurt.

Someone knocked on the back door.

Clara and I giggled nervously.

The door opened, David walked into the kitchen and sat down at the table in a chair next to mine. "I wanted to see you before you took off for work."

"Would you like me to explain what happened yesterday?" I asked.

He looked at my hands, then gently covered them with his. In a low voice I had never heard before, he said, "I just wanted to see for myself that you two are all right. I know some of the story. You can fill me in on the rest tonight. Now, off to work you go." His chin quivered a bit. He left quickly out the back door.

I didn't want him to leave. I wanted to grab his sleeve and pull him back, and spend some time with him alone. Alone with David would have been heaven. But he was right as usual—it was time for us to head out to Denise's and then over to the Staley Mansion.

After I dropped off Clara, I sped over to the ocean view neighborhoods of Aptos and was surprised to see Chester's truck parked at the Staley house. A minute later, three of his employees arrived in two more pickups. Feeling happy that my friend had finally come back to work, I climbed out of my truck.

Someone honked behind me.

I twirled around, and flattened myself against the side of my truck.

Rod aimed his truck as close to me as he could without actually hitting me. Wearing an evil grin, the only grin he owned, he rolled up behind Chester's truck and tapped it on the back bumper lightly.

Two more pickups pulled to a stop in the middle of the driveway and four of Rod's workers climbed out. Six trucks plus my pickup and Alicia's SUV filled most of the driveway. Because of rough talk from Rod and his four swaggering workmen, Alicia and I decided to hunker down in her car until the coast was clear.

Ponce handed a baseball bat to Rod.

Chris and a couple of roofers sat down in the green grass of the Staley's immaculate lawn, ready to watch a good fight. Chester and his three hired guys stood near the koi pond discussing the day's work plan. Chester ignored Rod until the man came too close for comfort. Rod puffed up his chest, telling Chester to leave the property or he would have to use the bat.

The Staleys stood on the front steps, ready to call the police if needed.

Chester ducked as the baseball bat came his way, but the second swing glanced off his handsome head, leaving a small gash. He grabbed the end of the bat, wrenched it out of Rod's hands and tossed it into the pond.

Rod's guys moved in closer.

Twenty feet away from the fight, Alicia and I shouted through the Volvo windshield, rooting for our favorite guy. Naturally, our money was on Chester. We yelled and screamed; but every time anyone came close to the Volvo, we rolled up the windows and locked the doors.

Rod tried to provoke our friend into a fight by calling him every nasty name he could think of. In his frustration, he took a few swings at Chester, but his fist never connected. Finally, Rod grabbed Chester's ponytail and pulled him to the ground.

Big mistake! Our guy was furious. He pulled Rod down to his knees then gave him an upper-cut square in the nose.

Rod went face down into the grass, holding his nose, shrieking. He finally raised his head and looked at Chester. "You broke my nose!"

The Staleys went back inside.

Everyone walked away.

Alicia and I ran to help Chester.

Rod was obviously hurting. He dove into his truck and burned rubber leaving the scene.

Alicia stayed with Chester while I ran to the house for a wet cloth and bandages. Liana had been watching from the window. She opened the door for me and handed over a first aid box and a wet hand towel. When Chester's head was clean and bandaged, we gave him our estimate of his condition.

"You bled a lot," I said, "but heads do that."

"I don't think you need stitches," Alicia said, "but we can drive you to the hospital if you like."

"Don't think I'll go to the hospital, but thanks anyway. That's probably where Rod will be for the next couple hours. I'll be fine," he reassured us.

Chester called his workmen together to finish their discussion about the day's work. As we were crossing the lawn, I heard Chester say that he and another fellow would be installing copper panels. But to start off, he gave each man an outside job. While his men were busy, he went inside and miraculously conjured up the boxes of missing copper panels.

All morning Liana acted like a child in a candy store on a sugar high, flitting around the house, inspecting progress on the library ceiling, then back to the almost finished Chop Suey mural. Herbert followed her everywhere as usual. Liana's enthusiasm was contagious. We felt it as we poured our hearts into the finishing touches of the painting.

Mid-morning, I took a short break, walked down the hall and watched Chester installing the panels. His helper made the job go twice as fast. They talked about the fight and laughed so hard I thought they might fall off their ladders.

Liana stood with me watching Chester, his head bandaged, his strong arms tapping panels into place. Obviously, it would be several days before they finished. In the meantime, a security company was scheduled to come to the house to give an estimate. For security reasons, Chester and the Staleys thought it best that the work continue over the weekend. Once the panels were installed, they would be hard to steal. And a new security system would make sure everything was safe.

Liana turned and walked out of the library.

I followed her.

"Liana, what do you think touched off the fight today?"

"Sometimes men need to let off steam. Yesterday we fired Rod for the second time, so he had a lot of steam to let go of. I'm just sorry that Chester was injured."

"He seems to be fine and working hard. Liana, I'd like to know why Rod was fired." I suddenly felt the need to justify my curiosity about Rod, so I added, "My aunt and Denise and I had a horrific experience yesterday. We almost burned up in a house fire...."

"Oh no! You poor dears! I read about the Garrett house in *The Sentinel* this morning. Don't tell me you were there."

"We were locked in the basement, and we literally clawed our way out." I showed her my fingers and fingernails.

"Oh, that's dreadful!" Liana uttered.

"Eddie Garrett had rented his basement to Rod," I said, "who crammed it full of hardware, tools, you name it. But yesterday, everything was gone, just a big empty basement with new locks on the door. Someone left the door unlocked, so naturally we went inside to look around."

"Naturally," Liana said.

"As soon as we were inside, someone padlocked the door. We clawed at a mouse hole, eventually making it big enough to crawl through."

Liana's eyes widened. "Seriously, you did that? A mouse hole?" She took another look at my hands. "I wonder...we fired Rod because he bought materials and tools for the garden wall project, but he charged us for things he didn't use or even need. Lloyd confronted him about the matter, but he just stormed out of here."

"Liana, I wish you had seen the basement before it was emptied. There were all kinds of new tools that looked like they had never been used. I remember seeing half a dozen shiny new shovels against the wall; and I saw three new generators, several chainsaws and about twenty buckets of nails. And one of Eddie's bedrooms was full of new stuff, like tools, pipes and faucets."

"Sounds like we may have to go to court..." Liana mumbled.

Around noon, my painters and I had a little powwow where we critiqued the mural and talked about a few minor details such as a few stronger highlights and shadows. It looked like we might be able to go home early. Kyle put finishing touches on his waiter, and Alicia changed the color of a lady's hat from orange to purple. The Chop Suey painting had sucked us into the roaring twenties, where flappers flapped and bathtub gin was the drink of choice.

Lloyd hung out in the dining room for a while. "This painting makes me feel like I should have a Stutz Bearcat or a Duesenberg parked in my garage. The nineteen twenties must have been a great time to be alive."

"Yeah, if you had lots of money," Kyle said.

"You're right, son. People without money had a hard life," Lloyd agreed.

"Some things never change," Alicia added.

"It's only three o'clock," I said, "but I think we can pack up and you two can go home. The painting looks finished...what do you think, Mr. Staley?"

"I think it's top drawer—wonderful really. I only wish it had been my idea," he chuckled. "You'll be painting the garden wall next?"

"That's the plan," I said. "I'll apply the undercoat this afternoon." I folded one tarp, then another. "Where would you like us to store our equipment?"

"The storage room in the basement would be a good place," he said.

When everything had been hauled down to the basement and the dining room furniture had been arranged back to its normal configuration, Alicia and Kyle went home. I stayed two more hours, rolling primer on the garden wall. A little after five, I drove over to Denise's apartment and knocked on the door.

"Come in, Josephine," Denise beamed.

I stepped inside. "Your mural is fantastic! I love that big old octopus…and the shark! He looks hungry. What's that in his mouth?"

Denise smiled, "A piece of pink polka dot bikini."

"That's what I thought it looked like. Whose idea was that?"

She looked over at Clara.

"Auntie, this is a side of you I don't know."

My aunt snickered. "Growing up in Santa Cruz, I envied those little beach girls in their bathing suits. Actually, your mother was one of them. Funny how Leola always 'fit in' and I didn't. But I love my life the way it is now," Clara said, "especially when I can paint a shark with a bikini in his mouth."

Denise laughed a strangled kind of laugh. I could almost feel her childhood pain—pain and sadness that had extended into her adult life.

"That's one more thing your aunt and I have in common." Denise looked at me, "I bet you 'fit in,' Josephine."

"Actually, I did fit in with three other girls from my art classes. We took art every year for the fun of it. What they didn't understand was that even though I was having fun, I was completely serious about my art.

I'm a lot like Aunt Clara. I love my life. I love painting for a living."

"What happened to your three friends?" Denise asked.

"They work as secretaries."

Clara rolled her eyes. "Personally, I would have loved to have had a career like Denise's. I like lots of action."

"Auntie, you would have loved it over at the Staley's today. Rod and Chester got into a fight. Rod went off to the hospital, and Chester didn't look too good either. Plenty of action."

"Speaking of action," Denise said, "Ben's coming home tonight." She winked at Clara. "Let's celebrate the new mural with a nice dinner, my treat."

"And we finished our mural in the dining room today," I added. "We'll make a toast to Ben and the two murals."

Denise organized her jars of paint while Clara folded the tarps. I washed brushes. The cleaning brushes job was endless in my world. Oh well...what's a few more brushes?

When all the paint equipment had been stashed in the hall closet and the ladder lowered into its usual place on the little deck outside, we clambered into Denise's gray mid-size Ford sedan, Clara in the front, me in the back. Her car showed no wear whatsoever.

"Denise, how old is your car?"

She took a moment to count the years. "Eight years old this month."

"It looks brand new," Clara said.

"I'm thinking of trading it in for something..."

"Red," I said.

"Sporty," Clara said.

"How did you know?" Denise laughed.

"Shall we go to the Village Pub?" Aunt Clara asked.

"Great idea," Denise answered.

Chapter 20

At six o'clock, The Village Pub was dead quiet. Half an hour later, the place had turned into a circus, raising the noise level exponentially. A card game, ignored by management, started up at the table in the far corner with Myrtle dealing. The bar was shoulder to shoulder with sweaty workmen and a couple of ladies in summer frocks.

Our little table was central to everything.

Myrtle waved to us from her table, and Fred stopped by to say, "Howdy."

Rod and his right-hand man, swaggered in.

The waitress stood next to my chair. "How can I help you, ladies?"

"I have a question," I said. "See the big guy in the black t-shirt?" I pointed to Rod sitting at the bar.

She nodded.

"Was he here last night?"

"I can't really say…"

"Yes, you can. It's a matter of life and death."

She took a step back and looked at me like I had fallen off my pogo stick.

Clara said, in a calmer voice, "My dear, we're asking for vital information pertaining to a serious crime. It could save a life."

"Well, I think he came in at six or seven… Would you like something to drink?"

"We'll try your best brown ale on tap," Denise said.

"The last time I drank beer," Clara said, "was over thirty years ago at a baseball game. While my husband was buying beer and peanuts, our friend's beeper beeped and he had to leave. I drank the beer that was meant for him. It was pretty good, as I recall. The second one was delicious."

"Was it Ben…?" Denise asked.

"Oh, no, it was my first husband. He died years ago. I've been married to Ben for less than a year now."

"What about you, Josephine? I notice you wear a diamond ring."

"My first husband was killed seventeen years ago by an eighteen-wheeler. Now I'm engaged to David Galaz, my neighbor… These fries are the best, don't you think?"

"I ordered the bangers and mash," Clara said, "so I'll have to dip into your basket of fries."

"No problem, Auntie, help yourself. You too, Denise."

"Actually, I'm watching my figure…" Denise admitted.

"Is there a lucky guy watching it too?" Clara asked.

"Oh, I don't know…" Denise focused on the ale in front of her.

Clara leaned closer to Denise in a confidential way. "Buy that red sporty car. It'll work like a guy magnet. You'll have dozens of men to choose from."

"But I only want…ah, the salt, please."

Changing the subject, I asked Denise if she would be going back to work soon. She said she was scheduled to go back on Monday. She and Sayer would be covering Aptos and Soquel in the cruiser.

"This might sound funny," Denise said, "but I feel like a different person. I just hope it lasts."

"You'll be fine, dear, no matter what happens. Just remember that happiness is a choice, and you have chosen to be happy. You have a pretty smile, so use it."

"Thank you for everything, Clara..." Denise's eyes looked ready to overflow. She squared her shoulders and took a deep breath. "I couldn't have made it this far without you."

When my fish and chips were gone, I excused myself from the table to go speak to Myrtle. She had already had a winning streak, judging by the pile of matchsticks in front of her. Fred saw me and began to chat. Myrtle finally looked up and smiled. Boy could she shuffle a deck of cards.

"Okay, gentlemen, I'm taking a break," Myrtle announced, stood up and walked with me to our table. I helped her into an empty chair, and Denise ordered a beer for Myrtle and another one for Aunt Clara.

"Oh, here comes Freddy," Myrtle said.

Denise pulled over a chair from another table.

Fred sat down. He dipped fries into catsup and proceeded to paint his white beard red. Myrtle grabbed a paper napkin and wiped his whiskers. He smiled as she worked on his beard. They were obviously VERY good friends.

Five frothy steins arrived.

"You ladies are looking lovely as ever," Fred said, his eyes following the waitress in her tight black outfit and white apron. When his elderly eyes finally came back to us, he asked, "Ladies, anything exciting going on in your lives?"

"Yesterday was...unusual," Clara said. "We were trapped in a burning building and barely made it out in time."

Fred threw his head back and laughed. "That's a good one, Clara!"

"We're thankful for every day given to us," she said. My aunt drained her stein and licked her lips. "What time did Ben say he would be at your house, Josephine?"

"I think he said around eight-thirty. We should head home soon."

"Yes, dear, I hope I'm not tipsy when Ben sees me." Clara stood up slowly, testing her balance. Watching her brought on a flashback of myself when I was eight-years-old, staggering up the aisle of a school bus, trying to tell the substitute driver that he had passed my stop. I remember being so embarrassed when he stopped the bus, and I fell forward flat on my face in the aisle.

Clara made it to the car safely, and Denise drove us back to her place. Clara and Denise hugged and cried and hugged some more. They exchanged phone numbers and finally parted.

Driving home, I asked Clara what she thought about the waitress' answer to my question about Rod.

"If he came to the pub at six, he couldn't have been the one; but if he came to the pub at seven, he might be the one who torched the house."

"Okay, peeling back the onion," I said, "someone loaded all that stuff into large U-Drive trucks, according to Denise. They probably had to take at least two, maybe three loads. We know that Rod was renting the space from Eddie, but how many people knew about all that junk?"

"Rod's hired help knew," Clara said. "Maybe they stole it from Rod."

"If that's the case, he sure looked calm and collected tonight at the pub."

"Josephine, dear, you missed the exit onto the freeway...."

"What about Bessie? Maybe she saw what happened." I made an illegal U-turn and headed back to Trout Gulch Road. "Don't worry, Auntie, we'll be home in plenty of time." My little truck roared up the curvy road. We turned onto Trickle Creek, zoomed past Eddie's driveway and parked in front of Bessie's house. She watched us from the porch where she sat with her cat sprawled across her lap.

"Hell-o!" Clara shouted as she hurried up the gravel drive, balancing herself side-to-side like an old biplane bomber coming in for a landing.

"Hello, yer self, my friend." Bessie pushed the cat off her lap and stood up.

I walked right behind my aunt, ready to catch her if she had trouble with the uneven ground. "Hello, Bessie," I said, as she clomped down the steps and hugged Clara.

"Would you like a glass ah water?" she asked my aunt.

"How sweet of you, yes, I would love one."

Bessie walked Clara up onto the porch, pulled out a chair for her, then disappeared into the house. She came back with two glasses of water, handed one to Clara and drank the other one herself. What was I, liverwurst?

"Bessie, what did you think yesterday when Eddie's house burned down?" I asked.

"I was worryin' about the forest, of course, and I worried that the fire might even burn its way up to my place. I loaded my two horses into their trailer, just in case we had to run for it."

"Did you happen to see anyone in the area around six o'clock?" Clara asked.

"Turn your head and look down the road. See anything?"

"I see what you mean," Clara said. "That curve in the road blocks the view. Do you have any idea who would have burned Eddie's place? The fire was set on purpose, and we were locked in the house."

"Oh dear, that's just awful! Well it looks like you come out okay…"

"Yes, but it was a close call," Clara sighed, looking down at her poor ravaged fingers. "I still can't believe someone would try to kill us."

"Maybe they didn't know you was in there. What was ya doin' in the basement anyway?"

"How did you know we were in the basement?" I asked.

"Just an edicated guess."

"Anyway, my fiancé is a close friend of the Garrett family," I explained, "and we have all been taking turns looking after the place."

Bessie nodded her head. "You won't have to do that no more."

"Bessie, would you mind if we looked at your horses? I just love horses…" Clara swooned.

Bessie glanced at the barn. "I would except that Brody's been doin' some work in the barn and it's all tore up. It's old and might fall…"

"That's okay, Bessie, maybe on another visit."

Bessie's jaw relaxed, and she smiled politely.

I told Bessie that we had to hurry home because Clara's husband would be arriving at my house very soon. We took our leave and this time I drove straight to Aromas, enjoying a red-going-purple sky and buttermilk clouds overhead.

Clara and I were just hauling our tired bodies out of the truck when David drove up my driveway and tooted the horn.

I walked over to his window, instantly feeling great. "What's going on?"

"Ben's crashed on the couch over at my place. I've been trying to call you. Don't you ever answer that cell phone?" he laughed.

"Why is Ben over there—Clara's dying to see him?"

"His plane actually arrived early. He said he was exhausted, and next thing I knew he's asleep on my couch."

Clara leaned closer to his window. "I can believe it, poor darling."

"See you over at my place," David said, as he backed his car down the driveway.

Clara and I fed the dogs and quickly changed into non-paint outfits, trying to look wonderful for our guys. It was worth the effort. Ben was full of funny stories, and the evening went smoothly until David got a call from Jimmy. After a long talk with his friend, who usually didn't talk much, David came back to the living room looking somber.

"Yesterday was a bad day for Fiona," David said, as he scrubbed his kitchen counters with a sponge. "Apparently Fiona was acting suicidal, threatening to jump off a bridge over the freeway. She had driven her Lamborghini onto the 101 and 680 interchange in San Jose, parked the car in the middle of traffic and walked over to the edge."

"Oh dear!" Clara gasped, both hands covering her mouth.

"As Fiona watched the traffic moving along the layers of crisscrossing exit ramps below, a gentleman grabbed her from behind. He talked to her and held her there until the Highway Patrol arrived.

"Poor dear," Clara said, "is she feeling better now?"

"I don't know. Fiona spent the night under observation, but they let her come home today. She will have to go to court at some point." David shook his head. "Like I said, they cited her, took her downtown to be evaluated, put her in the hospital overnight and let her go today. Jimmy said that Fiona wants to talk to you, Josie."

"We're not the best of friends, but I'll go see her first thing tomorrow morning."

"That's sweet of you," Clara said.

"We could drive over there now," David suggested.

"Tomorrow is soon enough. I'm so tired. A lot has happened this week," I said, snuggling closer to my guy on the couch.

"A lot happened this week—like what?" Ben asked, in a kind voice. "I understand that painting murals can be physically exhausting…"

I took a deep breath, "Denise, Clara and I were locked in Eddie's basement when the house was burning down. We barely made it out alive. The next day our friend, Chester, was injured in a fight with Rod…."

"Wow, let me get this straight, you gals were in Eddie's basement because?" Ben tilted his head to one side. "Whoever Eddie is…"

"You don't really care who Eddie was, do you?" Clara said, snuggling closer to Ben on the sofa. "I'm too tired to talk about it."

I tried Clara's technique, "David, I'm so tired, let's talk about it later."

"What's wrong with now?"

"Okay, what do you want to know?" I asked, trying not to sound completely sarcastic. I turned in my seat and said to Ben, "You don't know Eddie Garrett and Clara never met him either. We were sort of looking into his murder…."

Aunt Clara jumped in with, "The way I understand it, Eddie was a handyman and he used to work for David on occasion, like when he needed help with gophers..."

"Peculiar things were happening at Eddie's house," I explained. "Rod had rented Eddie's basement so he could store stuff...."

"And all that stuff was brand new. It filled the big old basement completely," Clara added.

"But yesterday we went with Sheriff Lund to check on Eddie's place and every single item was gone from the basement. Denise figured it had taken at least two, maybe three, large U-Drive trucks to get it all," I said.

The men stared at us in the way that Martians look at Venetians, even though we were being very clear with our explanations.

"So now that you know the whole story," I said, "Who do you think set fire to Eddie's house ?"

Big silence.

Finally Ben said, "Must be the guys in the U-Drive trucks."

"I'd like to know who told Fiona that Eddie's house had burned down...before it did," David said.

"Fiona could have made that up to get us over there." I squirmed in my seat, feeling like I needed a break from the Garrett problems...a day away, a ride in the country, anything. The guys quizzed us on every angle, but none of it helped to solve the mystery.

"On second thought, maybe we should visit Fiona. What if she goes back to the bridge...?" I yawned, "Anyone want to go?"

David looked relieved. "I think we need to go right away...besides, I sort of promised Jimmy I'd get you over to see her."

"We'll say goodbye now," Ben said. "We have a long drive home."

Clara nodded but didn't say a word. There were hugs and tears; but no words, just the ones that were stuck in our throats. The stars came out. Ben, Clara and Sara left, and David and I hit the highway going north on 101. As we moved along in light traffic getting closer to the Almaden side of San Jose, I looked up at various overpasses. Of course, I didn't see a red Lamborghini anywhere, thankfully, but I couldn't help looking. Five more miles and we were cruising the Almaden neighborhoods—so many well-kept older homes, tree-lined streets and a beautiful golf course— not that I could see much of it, being dependent on headlights and streetlights.

"Okay, we're here, my lovely," David said. One kiss, and we climbed out of the Miata. I stretched, yawned and tried to gather up some energy. It was almost ten o'clock. A big silver moon rose up behind us. We walked arm-in-arm along the sidewalk and a few steps up to the front door.

David rang the bell.

Jimmy cracked the door open. "Oh, it's you, come on in."

"Hey, Jimmy, how's it goin'?"

"Not too good, really," he said in a low voice, looking over his shoulder at a lump on the sofa in the next room. We moved into the living room. The lump moved, sat up and wanted to know who was at the door.

"It's David and Josephine, dear."

"You've got to be kidding...."

By that time, we were all standing in the spacious, professionally decorated living room. Fiona looked up at me in my ugly paint clothes, and I looked down at her red eyes and messy hair.

"Kinda late to be out visiting, isn't it?" she said.

The guys took off for the kitchen.

"I was ready to ring your neck yesterday...." I said.

"Go ahead, I don't have anything to live for."

"What do you mean by that? Jimmy's a great guy and you have a great life," I said. "Beautiful home, Lamborghini, what more do you need?"

"I...need, sob...to be...needed."

"Well, I know for a fact that Jimmy needs you. And what's that got to do with what you did to me, telling me that Eddie's house had burned down? There were three of us in that house. We were locked inside and barely escaped being burned alive. I'd love to know why you're involved in this kind of thing."

"I promised...."

"You promised what?" It was all I could do to keep from slapping her face.

"I was just doing my civic duty, helping the homeless."

"Give me a break..."

"You don't understand, Josephine, I'm on the San Jose City Council, among other things. For the last two years, we've been building a series of small homes, just four-hundred-square feet each. The land was donated, and a lot of people donate their time and talent building these tiny homes. I was able to help by supplying the workers with building materials at a very low cost."

"And how were you able to do that?" I asked, already guessing where this boat was going.

"Eddie rented his basement to someone for storage. The renter acquired all kinds of tools and supplies and sold them to us, through Eddie, cheap. Eddie did it as a favor, to help the homeless. He said he didn't keep any of the money—just the rent money." Fiona hiccupped and wiped her nose with a Kleenex.

"So how does that explain what you did to me?" I growled.

"I had arranged for a large shipment of supplies to be delivered last month." Her bottom lip quivered. "I sent Eddie the check to give to his renter. The shipment never came, but the check was cashed. The Council has been hounding me, and I don't know how to get the money back or get the supplies since Eddie is dead, and I don't know who the renter is."

"Whom did you write the checks to?"

"No one, I always left them blank—just the amount and the date, and signed my name, of course," she sniffled.

"Did you ever question where all this hardware was coming from?"

Fiona stared at the floor. "I was afraid the stuff might have been stolen, so I purposely didn't want to know who I was dealing with."

"So you made yourself look good to the committee...."

"But it did help the homeless," she argued.

"So who told you that Eddie's house burned down, and then told you to tell me?"

Fiona was silent.

I still wanted to slap her, but not as hard as before.

Chapter 21

Something about Saturday morning put me on edge. My house was way too quiet, no roar from the vacuum cleaner, no perking coffee, no one to talk to except Solow, and he was looking miserable because Sara had gone home. Lying in bed, I thought about my visit with Fiona. She was in a tight spot, but she had put herself there, wanting to be a big shot with the City Council. I didn't have any answers for her predicament, and she didn't have all the answers I wanted from her. All she could tell me was that a man with a deep voice had called her and told her that she had been dealing with stolen merchandise. He said he would keep her activities quiet if she would do one favor for him. All she had to do was call me and report that Eddie's house had burned to the ground.

Fiona said she hadn't known it was a lie.

"Did the man speak with an accent?" I asked.

"No, I would have remembered that."

It had become obvious that someone was after me, saw that I was getting close to finding something important and wanted me out of the way. Just because he didn't succeed, didn't mean he wouldn't try again. I would have to be very careful...but being careful usually went contrary to the circumstances in my complicated life.

David came over for a visit around noon. Thankfully, he had given me time to sleep late, call Mom, pay the bills and put them in the mailbox. We hadn't gotten home until midnight Friday from Jimmy and Fiona's house in San Jose, making it a very long day for me. But Saturday morning was progressing in a positive way. I was happy to finally have some quality time with my guy.

"Josie, do you think your folks would like some of my homemade apricot salsa?"

"Does Solow like bacon? Of course they would love some salsa. I plan to make brownies this afternoon. They'll be a break from Mom's banana bread. I told her I was bringing them, so maybe she won't feel like she has to bake."

"How are the folks?" he asked.

"Mom sounded good on the phone, but Myrtle hinted that Mom has some kind of problem, and I should go see her soon. Myrtle's been acting very mysterious lately, not to mention being out of control with her gambling."

"You mean Bingo?"

"No, poker."

David looked stunned for a minute, then laughed.

His cell phone rang. He answered it.

Solow followed me around the house hoping for a walk in the neighborhood because he was bored silly without Sara.

"All right, let's put on your leash and go for a walk..."

"David here. No kidding. Don't worry, Jimmy, she probably went shopping." But I knew David was worried by the sound of his voice. They hung up, and Solow and I went for our walk. When we got back, David was on the phone with Jimmy again.

Had I been too hard on Fiona last night? Was it my fault she wasn't at home? Poor Jimmy; it sounded like he was going crazy looking for her. David did his best to keep his friend calm.

"Josie, honey, I'm going to run over to Jimmy's."

"I'll go with you."

On the way to San Jose, I had second thoughts. How could we help Fiona anyway? But, on the other hand, I needed to support David and that meant being there for his friends. Almaden was green and clean—a lovely place to live if you liked organized neighborhoods. But I had been a country girl way too long to appreciate sidewalks and close neighbors.

David parked the Miata at the curb, and we walked arm in arm up to Jimmy and Fiona's front door. No one answered the doorbell.

David snooped around, peeking in windows, while I waited at the door.

He came back looking puzzled. "The last time I talked to Jimmy, he said he would be home if I wanted to come over."

"Did you look in the garage window?" I asked.

"Yeah, he took the Harley. I'll try calling him." He punched in the number. "Hey, Jimmy, where are you?"

"I'm cruising around; I couldn't stay home and do nothing. Where are you?"

"Josephine and I are at your house…"

"I'll be home in five minutes." Jimmy hung up.

In less than five minutes, Jimmy was home having a soda with David.

"Sweetheart, would you mind if I take the Miata to the drug store? I need to buy, ah, something."

"Here's the key, Josie."

Thankfully, there were no more questions. I put the little Miata into gear and left the neighborhood. I had no idea where to go to find Fiona, but like Jimmy, I just had to be out there looking. I figured the red Lamborghini would be easy to spot, if I happened upon it. But San Jose was a big town, stretching for miles in every direction. I changed the radio station to music I liked and entered Highway 101 heading south. Traffic was moving at a steady five miles per hour with frequent stops. The music ended and the news came on. The first item was a warning not to take Highway 101 south because there was a problem at the interchange with Highway 680, a possible copycat jumper.

The "jumper" word sent shivers down my spine. The radio report had been too late for me. I was already headed up the 680 ramp, a hundred feet above a crisscross of highway exit ramps.

I skirted around several vehicles idling in the double-lane, one-way overpass.

Crossing the bridge turned out to be slower than driving under it. Police and Highway Patrol cars were arriving and parking all over the overpass. I squeezed the little Miata between a couple of cop cars but in the end, I was blocked at both ends. I turned off the engine and watched from my driver's seat as a policewoman talked to a blond wearing a yellow tank top, red shorts and alligator cowboy boots. The middle-aged woman had one leg over the three-foot high concrete ledge and was threatening to jump.

Two policemen standing near the Miata discussed the woman's desire for something to drink. I plucked a bottle of water from the console, climbed out of the car and walked about twenty feet over to the woman in red shorts who was now sitting on the edge with both legs dangling.

"Hi, there," I said, in my most casual voice.

The policewoman glared at me.

"I heard that this lady wants something to drink," I said.

Ms. Policewoman put a hand up to keep me from coming any closer.

The blond shifted her body around and smiled when she saw the bottle of water.

"If you come this way a bit," I said, "I'll meet you and you can have the water."

The officer's mouth dropped open as she stepped back and let the gal walk over to me. Police from every direction formed a circle around us as the poor irrational, obviously unstable woman gulped water from a plastic bottle. She reminded me of a wild animal being restrained and held in captivity. But at least she wouldn't have another opportunity to jump for a while.

I asked one of the officers if I could be allowed to leave the scene. I told him I was prone to having a fear of heights. He took my name and particulars and said I might have to answer questions at a later date. I promised I wouldn't travel out of the country any time soon. He voluntarily moved his SUV closer to the cluster of police cars so that I had just enough room to squeeze by and continue over the 680 bridge.

When I arrived at Jimmy's house, I was happy to see the garage door open and a red Lamborghini parked inside. I entered the front room where everyone sat eating popcorn, eyes trained on the US Open Golf Tournament at Pebble Beach on TV. I sat down beside David. They barely knew I was there. I found out later that Fiona had taken a six-hour joyride up to the wine country in Lodi because she had run out of her favorite Merlot. She bought a couple cases of it and drove home.

David and I said our goodbyes and headed for home around three o'clock. If I hurried, I would be able to bake a batch of brownies from my very reliable brownie recipe that Aunt Clara had given me years ago.

David dropped me at my house because I asked him to. If he hadn't gone home, I would have been completely unable to keep track of the ingredients I put in the brownie dough. He was a chick magnet and I was his chick—simple as that! I went to work immediately, pulling out a multitude of ingredients and a bowl to put them in. But my mind was on Fiona's predicament, no matter how hard I tried to focus on baking brownies.

Most of the ingredients were in the bowl when the phone rang. I picked up my cell phone from the table. It was Mom wondering when we would be leaving to go to Santa Cruz. She didn't sound like her confident and upbeat self.

"What's the matter, Mom?" I asked, stirring batter with my other hand. Normally I would have a finger full of batter to taste, but not this time. I scraped the thick batter into a baking pan while pressing the phone against my ear with my shoulder.

The phone dropped into the batter.

I put the bowl down and plucked the phone out of the dark chocolatey goo.

"Mom, are you there?"

I wiped sticky batter off the phone with a wet paper towel.

"Mom, are you there?"

"Hello...Josephine? I think we have a bad connection, dear."

"It's okay now. My phone works. Now, what is it you're worried about?"

"Who, me, worried?"

"We'll talk when I get there," I said. "Gotta run." We hung up. I shoved the brownie pan into the preheated oven and began cleaning the kitchen. When that was done, I went through the messages on the old message machine. One message had my curiosity up. Fiona said someone had called her and wanted to deliver the building materials. All she had to do was bring another couple hundred dollars in cash. She asked me to call her.

Fiona picked up on the first ring. "Thank you for calling, Josephine." Her voice trembled. "Like I said, someone wants to deliver the materials tonight, at midnight. What should I tell them?"

"Tell them, yes, and call the cops and let them take care of it."

"I can't exactly do that...remember when I told you that I take care of my mother when she's sick? Well, the guy said he knows where my mother lives. It sounded very ominous. I'm so scared...."

"Hang on a second Fiona, my timer just went off." I put the phone down, grabbed a potholder and pulled the brownie pan out of the oven.

"Sorry, Fiona, what is it you want me to do?"

"I haven't exactly told Jimmy everything yet, but I will...but I was wondering if you could come to the construction project in south San Jose tonight so that I don't have to open the gate by myself. Jimmy would call the police, but I'm afraid for my mother."

"How can you go there in the middle of the night without Jimmy knowing?"

"That's easy; I always sleep in the guest room when I have a migraine. I'll tell him I have a headache, and he won't hear me get up and leave. Josephine, take down this address—2200 East Monroe, San Jose."

"I'll look at my old maps," I told her. "I have quite a collection."

Fiona gave me her cell number and a few more details, thanked me and hung up.

What was I thinking? I had just promised to drive forty miles in the middle of the night to do what? Help Fiona open a gate?

I located my little spray can of pepper spray and tossed it into my purse—just in case. My flashlight and driving directions were next to go into the purse.

A knock on the front door startled me out of the midnight madness thoughts. I opened the door.

"David, don't tell me it's time to go already."

"Fraid so," he laughed, as I darted away to the bathroom for a quick clean-up. When I came back with hair combed and lipstick on, David had already put foil over the brownie pan and fed Solow his kibble.

The night was chilly. Fog had moved inland, smothering Aromas with misty wetness. Not enough wetness for an umbrella—just enough to keep faces cold and damp. Just enough moisture to require putting on the wipers manually every twenty seconds. But I wasn't driving, so I relaxed, hoping to have a little catnap before my midnight rendezvous with Fiona. The sound of David's voice drifted away.

Sometime later, David shook my shoulder.

I looked up into his magnificent brown eyes, but he didn't want a kiss. He just wanted to point out the fact that we were parked in front of Mom and Dad's place. We were about twenty-five feet from the house and could barely see the front door. Obviously, Santa Cruz fog was thicker than Aromas fog. Dad stood in the doorway looking like a wispy shadow and sounding like a distant foghorn with his greeting. A minute later, I was in his arms, glad to be in the house of my youth.

Mom hugged me while David carried the brownie pan to the kitchen. I had intended to arrange the brownies on a pretty plate but didn't have time.

"Mom, what's that on your thumb?"

She held up her right thumb wrapped in gauze. "It's nothing, dear, just a poke from a rose thorn."

"Isn't that the same hurt thumb as last week? Why does your right hand look bigger than your left hand?"

"Like I said, just a poke from a thorn," she shrugged.

Dad stepped closer. "Don't get the wrong idea; Leola has been fighting this thing for over two weeks."

"What does the doctor say?" David asked.

Dad cleared his throat. "Gave her some medicated salve two weeks ago."

"Let's all sit down in the living room," Mom said, leading the way. When we were situated on the couch with Dad in his recliner, she said, "Actually, my thumb is getting better. Myrtle suggested I soak it in hot water and Epsom salts. Good thing she lives right next door."

I heard the back door slam.

"Speaking of Myrtle, here she is," Dad said, as Myrtle carefully walked through the kitchen and dining room, into the living room carrying a bag of Oreo cookies, her contribution to the dinner.

"Lovely to see you, Josephine, David," she said, as she dropped into Mom's favorite overstuffed chair, cookies, purse and all.

"Myrtle's been spending a lot of time at her sister's house in Aptos," Mom said. "We don't see her very often these days."

Myrtle gave me a one-second warning glance. "My sister's been ailing a bit, so we think we should spend more time together since we're both getting older."

Even though Myrtle was only one year older than my folks, she looked and acted decades older.

The selection of clothes in her closet hadn't changed in over forty years, at least. She said she was determined to wear the clothes out before she died—get her money's worth. It looked to me like most of the items were well past the "spoil date."

Dad excused himself to go look at the meat in the oven. He came back and sat down but a few minutes later left to go toss the salad.

"Dad, do you need help in the kitchen…?" I asked.

He said everything was under control, not to worry.

Suddenly the smoke alarm in the kitchen went off.

I looked at Mom. She rolled her eyes to the ceiling and held up her right hand wrapped in gauze.

I came from a fairly traditional family. Mom usually cooked the food and Dad usually cleaned up the kitchen after dinner. But at that moment, Dad was racing around the house, opening windows and doors, trying to get the alarm to stop. Food was burning somewhere in the kitchen, and he didn't want help from me, not that I was Martha Stewart or anything.

David stood up, "I'll be right back," he said.

We didn't see David again until the meal was served. The men had done a wonderful job—every morsel was divine. The table was set just right, including roses from the garden, the good dishes and silver and two choices of wine.

Myrtle bowed her head. Her wig moved forward slightly. She said grace, and then we dug into a delicious meal. Myrtle talked about many things but never mentioned her real activities in Aptos, so I didn't bring up the Village Pub, although I really wanted to. I had questions. But maybe the questions would all be answered during the upcoming midnight madness with Fiona in San Jose.

Dad stood up and announced that Leola had been unable to bake banana bread for desert because of her thumb, but we would have brownies and Oreo's instead. David cleared the plates away while Dad prepared five small bowls of vanilla ice cream, each crowned with one cookie and one brownie. The rest of the cookies and brownies were displayed on a large dish in the middle of the table.

Mom bit into her brownie. "Ugh!"

Myrtle bit into her brownie. "Oh my God!"

I tried a small bite of brownie and spit it into my napkin. It was more bitter than anything I had ever tasted. Bar soap tasted better than my brownies. I thought back to making the batter. I couldn't remember scooping, pouring or measuring sugar. I remembered the phone call, but there was no recollection of sugar. The brownie bust was my fault. I said I was sorry, and everyone said things like, "Oh, I've done that before, don't feel bad." But I couldn't help feeling bad anyway.

David and I gave Dad a little break and cleaned the kitchen for him. When we came back to the living room, Dad was snoring in his chair.

Myrtle stood up to leave, saying she had to go check on her sister.

I couldn't help it when my eyes rolled up to look at the ceiling.

Myrtle gave me a wink and ducked out of the house through the back door.

Mom sat on the sofa with her hand immersed in hot Epsom salts water, wishing us a safe trip home.

Chapter 22

All the way home, I had been trying to come up with an excuse to go to bed early. I wasn't about to tell David about my plan to meet Fiona at midnight in a new tract of little half-built homes for the homeless somewhere in the one hundred and eighty square miles of San Jose. I would need to spend time with a map.

"Josie, you're quiet tonight," David said, as we rolled through Aromas.

"Yeah, I guess so. Just a little worried about Mom. I don't understand why she's taking so long to heal."

"Her age might have something to do with it," he said.

"You're right. I always think of Mom and Dad as being indestructible." I yawned. The car rolled to a stop behind my truck. We could barely see the house through the fog. David cut the engine and put an arm over my shoulders. We unbuckled our seatbelts, kissed and climbed out of the car. We were instantly engulfed in a cool, wet and comforting cloud—a sweet sensation—like being under Grandma's feather comforter in her lumpy spring-loaded bed.

So far, I had not come up with a good excuse to go to bed early.

David walked me to the door. I opened it and Solow howled with happiness. He ran outside for a quick pee and then back to us for lots of petting and ear rubs. David held me tight and apologized for having to go home early. He said he had plumbing problems in the kitchen. He had turned off the water and took the pipes apart earlier in the day, but then we drove to San Jose and then it was time to go to Santa Cruz so he left everything for later. Now it was later and he had to fix the pipe so that he could turn the water back on.

"So, was that the plumbing problem you and Dad were talking about?"

"Yeah, your dad was a big help. I think I know how to solve the problem."

"Call a plumber?"

He laughed. "You know I'm a do-it-yourself guy, mostly."

I tried to look unhappy that he was leaving. Under different circumstances, I would have loved to have him stay. But not that night! We engaged in a long wonderful goodnight kiss, and then he and the little Miata disappeared into the mist.

It was already ten-thirty, and I had planned to leave for San Jose at eleven since I didn't know the town very well. In daylight I could get my bearings by looking at the golden hills on the east side of town and green mountains on the west side. I would be clueless in the dark. What kind of people delivered goods at midnight? —Nefarious nobodies, in my estimation. And why did Fiona want me to help her? Didn't she have any friends?

Too bad Sara had already gone home. I could have used her large fierce-looking presence as a backup to Solow and my can of pepper spray. Not that I was scared, just careful.

I grabbed a jacket, my purse and Solow's leash. He was happy to be going somewhere. I wished I had his attitude. The cab of my truck was warm and Solow quickly fell asleep. I tried not to think about sleep, but I had had a long day and I was tired. The coastal fog cleared away as we entered Highway 101 going north. Traffic was light. I checked my instructions for the zillionth time and turned onto San Felipe Road.

East Monroe wasn't as easy to find since San Felipe had no streetlights. I read and reread a couple miles worth of road signs, but I wasn't worried about being late. We had made better time than expected. I finally found East Monroe and soon after that, we were parked across the street from 2200.

We were fifteen minutes early. I turned off the engine and headlights, let my head rest on the back of the seat and relaxed. A three-quarter moon was rising off to my right, giving me a pretty good look at the rows of half-built little homes. My eyelids felt heavy.

Sometime later, Solow barked one quick bark.

I straightened up and looked around. It took a minute for me to figure out where I was and why. Across the street, a large-size U-Drive truck idled at the gate. Someone dressed in black came out of the dark, walked up to the gate and pushed the code buttons. The gate slid to one side. The U-Drive pulled into a sizable fenced in, paved area. Bordering the fenced area was empty land on all sides. No city lights—not even country lights, except for the massive clusters of lights a few miles away in the foothills.

A man climbed down from the front seat of the U-Drive.

Moments later a woman's shriek cut through the night air.

It had to be Fiona. Solow ran across the street with me, and through the gate. We crept up to the truck, feeling warmth from the tailpipe. I held onto Solow's collar and listened, as we moved quietly forward. I leaned against the right side of the U-Drive, and recognized Fiona's car parked a few yards away, sidled up to a big warehouse. I also recognized her voice.

"How do I know you didn't call the cops?" came a husky voice.

"Let go of my arm!" she demanded. "You'll just have to trust that I didn't tell anyone. Who are you anyway?"

"Shut up and hand over the money."

"You unload the truck first," she demanded.

"Money first."

Obviously, the transaction was not going well. I started backing away, pulling Solow toward the gate.

"Hand over the money..."

"Here, take it..." she hissed.

"Now, give me your purse."

"What? Are you crazy?" she shouted at him.

I heard a scuffle and Fiona said, "Ouch, get your hands off me!"

Solow and I quietly crossed the road and climbed into my truck. I fired it up, drove across the street, through the open gate and parked at a slant between the chain-link fence posts. The bully stood in the glow of my headlights, shielding his eyes and growling at me for blocking his departure.

"Unload that truck!" Fiona demanded.

"Over my dead body!" he yelled.

I climbed over the console, opened the passenger door and gave Solow a push.

"Go, Solow! Go get the bad man," I whispered. With one more push, I was able to convince my sweet dog to leap out of the truck and go sniff the man's shoes." Go get him, Thor!" I yelled out the window.

"Thor, get away from me..." the man said, his voice moving into a high pitch.

"Get him, Thor!" I shouted again, trying to distract the man.

While Solow kept the man's attention, Fiona inched her way over to the driver's side of the U-Drive, climbed in and took the keys. From there, she ran to my truck and climbed in. Solow was at her heels. She pulled him in and he settled into the space under the dash.

Two clicks and the doors were locked.

"Stupid women!" the man grumbled.

"We have all night, smart man!" Fiona shouted out her window.

We watched as the man pulled out his phone. "Hey Bro, where are you? You said you'd help me unload this truck," he grumbled, swearing and kicking his front tire.

Fiona and I sat in my pickup snickering. We watched as he unloaded the truck one piece at a time. He pulled, pushed and dragged large siding panels, hefted heavy sacks of cement one at a time and five gallon buckets of paint one after another. He unloaded buckets filled with hardware and hand tools. The last item to come out of the back of the U-Drive was a large tarp full of smaller hardware items. He carried it like Santa carrying his sack of toys, and dumped it unceremoniously on the pavement with everything else.

Fiona threw the U-Drive keys toward the empty truck.

I fired up my truck and made a quick getaway, before the man had time to follow us and make more trouble. I drove down San Felipe about a mile, then turned around and came back to the homes for the homeless. The gate was wide open, and the U-Drive was gone. As I braked in front of the pile of delivered goods, my headlights glommed onto what used to be a beautiful red Lamborghini.

A strangled cry came out of Fiona's mouth.

"Oh no!" I said, barely able to speak. Fiona's car had been crushed between the warehouse wall and a certain U-Drive. "Fiona, this is awful. You obviously can't drive…that, so I'll drive you home, but first we gotta get that jerk." I quickly backed up all the way to the street.

"Now close the gate! We're going after that creep!"

Fiona jumped out of the truck, locked the gate and climbed back in. "What do you plan to do?" she asked, her voice finally working again.

"Find him, then we'll think of something. I know what I would like to do to him, but I think there's a law against it." I poured on the gas once we were on San Felipe, heading south. My little pickup gobbled up the miles. Assuming the man had come from the Aptos area, I figured he would take Hecker Pass or Highway 129. I tossed a coin in my mind and decided on 129 since Hecker was steep and narrow. If I were driving a U-Drive, I would not want to drive Hecker Pass at night.

"Josephine, I think I should go home…"

"Sure, right after we crucify the creep."

We drove past Morgan Hill with no U-Drive in sight. We roared through Gilroy with no sign of the man. Once we left the freeway and continued on Highway 129, a two-lane road, there was little chance we would see the horrid truck and driver.

"I wonder if Jimmy knows I'm gone," Fiona said, breaking a long silence.

"If we don't find this guy before we get to Watsonville, I'll drive Hecker Pass to take you home." We would be making one huge circle through three counties.

"Josephine, slow down," Fiona said.

"Yeah, I see it. Looks like a wreck…"

"Looks like it just happened," Fiona said, as we pulled over and parked in the dirt behind the wreckage. "I smell smoke…oh no, flames!"

It looked like an SUV had pulled out of a side road and a passing U-Drive had nicked it. The SUV had twirled around until it pointed in the opposite direction. By the looks of it, the truck had leaped over a small gully and attacked a telephone pole on the other side.

The SUV woman ran up to us screaming that someone was trapped in the U-Drive. "I called 911," she said, "but I don't think they'll be here in time."

Fiona pulled the hysterical woman out of the road and sat her down in the grass. "Put your head down and take some deep breaths."

By that time, I was looking into the cab of the U-Drive, where a man sat with his bleeding head flopped on the steering wheel. I opened the door and tugged at his sleeve. He didn't move. Dead or alive, I was determined to get him out, but the grass had caught fire and was inching its way over to my feet.

"Fiona over here!" I shouted.

She left the woman and charged over to the truck. Fiona grabbed one arm. I had the other. Little flames were starting up on two sides of us. With all our strength, we yanked the man to the ground and dragged him over the grass onto the blacktop. It was more help than he deserved, but I couldn't help wishing him well. Fiona crouched down and listened for the man to breath.

"Eeuw! He's been eating garlic," she cringed.

"So, is he breathing?" I asked, still holding my own breath.

"Yes, he's breathing. I hope he doesn't die before he gets his jail jumpsuit."

"I'm glad he's breathing. He'll look great in orange."

Not only was he breathing, but an eye fluttered and almost opened.

"Tell us who your boss is," I demanded.

"Why should I?"

"Because I'm going to kill you if you don't..." Fiona said. The rest of what she said was drowned out by sirens coming closer—louder. Then it was quiet. Two firemen rushed toward us—one with a medical kit and one carrying a fire extinguisher.

More sirens headed our way, then silence. One Sheriff's car and a CHP vehicle parked along the roadside, red and blue lights twirling in the darkness of early morning.

Fiona approached the CHP officer. "Sergeant, I'm on the San Jose City Council, and we're working on a village for the homeless..."

"That's nice, now move over that way and let the EMT do his work."

"But officer, this man smashed my Lamborghini..."

"So you retaliated?" he said, pulling out a notepad.

"No, no we just followed him. He did this wreck on his own," Fiona said.

"Why do you think this man smashed your car?" he asked, pen at the ready.

"I was buying some things from him."

"In the middle of the night?"

"Well, yeah," she stammered. "He wanted more money than we had agreed on..."

"Ma'am, maybe you should speak to the Sheriff about your complaint." The CHP officer turned and walked over to the woman sitting in the grass with her SUV pointed in the wrong direction.

By that time, the injured man was plugged into air and fluids and his head had been wrapped. He was loaded onto a gurney, then into an ambulance. The shrill siren moved down the road and melted away as the boxy vehicle careened around the first turn, then another.

I walked up to the Sheriff and asked him what the injured man's name was because I wanted to send him a "Get Well" card.

"Ma'am, that is protected information. By the way, exactly what were you and your friend doing out here at this time of the night?"

"I was taking Fiona home, but I got a little bit lost."

"Your driver license says you live in Aromas. That's only three miles from here, and you were lost?"

"You know how you get turned around when it's dark. I don't usually drive when it's dark," I said, feeling my face flush with guilty lies.

Darkness deepened as the moon disappeared, and several rescue vehicles left the scene. Wispy fog began to encroach, moving eastward toward the hills. I shivered. My summer outfit was suddenly not enough against the chill.

"Josephine, the officer over there said we can leave now," Fiona said.

"Okay, let's do it." We clambered into the truck, barely interrupting Solow's sleep. I made a U-turn and we headed back to San Jose. Shortly after that, Solow's paws were twitching as he dreamt about Sara and Fluffy, I supposed. I wished I had time for a few dreams, but I had a lot of miles to drive before any dreams would be possible.

Fiona yawned.

"Don't do that," I said, and yawned.

"We'll talk, that will keep you awake," she said, and yawned again.

"Fiona, can you reach the bottle of water behind the seat?"

"Yep...got it." She took the lid off and handed the plastic bottle to me. I aimed and poured water down the front of my shirt.

Fiona gasped.

Chilled to the bone, I was suddenly awake. My mind kicked into high gear. Whoever took the building supplies from Eddie's basement had to have a warehouse of sorts to put the stuff in. Only one truckload was delivered to Fiona. Denise had estimated two or three truckloads would be necessary. Was the rest of the stuff being held somewhere else? After all my efforts, I still hadn't made a connection between the "stuff" and Eddie's murder.

Fiona's head leaned back and her eyes closed, but my mind was running in circles trying to come up with answers. A faint golden glow grew in the eastern sky. The sun would come up soon, and I hadn't even been to bed yet. I parked the truck in Fiona's short driveway. She woke up with a start.

"We're here already?" She yawned and climbed out of the cab but didn't close the door. She leaned in, "Josephine, why don't you come in and sleep on the couch? Solow is welcome too. That way you can be here in the morning when I tell Jimmy about my car. Besides, you're too tired to drive home. It wouldn't be safe."

"Thank you, Fiona. I think I'll take you up on that." Suddenly I felt exhausted. It was all I could do to make it to the couch and crash.

There were lots of crashes in my dreams. One of the crashes involved David's Miata heading north and an ocean liner heading south. There was a crash and the giant boat sank. Everyone aboard tried to climb onto and into David's car. He was angry because the crash wasn't his fault. After all, boats were not allowed on Highway 129.

Chapter 23

Sunday morning, almost noon, I opened my eyes and looked around. My first thought was, what is that heavenly smell? Solow wasn't in the room, so I rolled off the couch and went looking for him. Being a very smart dog, he had made his way to Jimmy and Fiona's kitchen, the source of the tempting aroma: pancakes and bacon. Fiona had actually given Solow his own plate of breakfast food.

"Good morning, Jo," she said, with no sign of attitude in her cheery voice.

"How many pancakes would you like?" Jimmy asked.

"Two, please," I said, curious about his good mood. Maybe Fiona hadn't told him about the Lamborghini? Breakfast was delicious and the conversation revealing to say the least. Apparently Fiona had already confessed to Jimmy everything that had happened, including the destruction of her car. From the sound of it, Jimmy never liked the car; and Fiona suddenly felt relieved that it was gone. They talked about possible replacement cars, all in the mid-size, mid-price range…like replacing crème brûlée with a tootsie roll.

We no sooner finished eating breakfast, than the San Jose Police arrived. Jimmy had called them earlier, reporting a hit and run on the Lamborghini. He and Fiona headed out to the scene of the crime with the cops, while I drove my brave basset home. I felt so proud of him and his part in our escape. But the questions lingered…who was that delivery guy, and who was he working for? I ran the whole scary scene over and over in my head. It had been too dark for me to see the man's face, and his hair was mostly covered with a baseball cap, but there was something about his voice—something familiar. The second time I saw him his face had been covered with blood.

Solow and I were home by two in the afternoon. The house was dead quiet without Clara around. I ran my messages—maybe she called me. Just the sound of her voice would help. I had three messages, but none from Aunt Clara. I showered, dressed and walked with Solow over to see David. We found him in the orchard sitting in a collapsible canvas chair, sound asleep with a BB gun on his lap.

"Hey, sweetums," I shook his shoulder.

David looked up and smiled. "Just trying to scare them," he laughed.

"I don't think a machine gun would scare these gophers."

"Don't be surprised if I take your suggestion," he laughed.

"Actually, I was thinking a drive in the country might be nice."

David waved his hand, "This is all country…."

"No, I mean forest, some place like Aptos."

"You want to go to Aptos on your day off?" He cocked his head and squinted one eye. But, eventually he drove me out to Eddie's property. There wasn't much to see, just smelly ashes and a few charred timbers.

"Thank goodness Eddie didn't have to see this happen," David mused.

"I guess it's Jimmy's property now," I said.

"Speaking of Jimmy, he called me today, before you came over. He told me how you and Solow saved

Fiona from 'who-knows-what last night.' I'm very proud of you, but I hope you girls never get into a situation like that again."

"I think Fiona learned a lesson last night. Did Jimmy tell you that she's resigning from the City Council? And she's going to replace her Lam with an ordinary economical car. When I saw her this morning, she was wearing her hair down and very little makeup, and her smile looked genuine. I'm really happy for them and for us, since we will probably be hanging out with them in the future.

David squeezed my shoulder. "You had a big part in all of that."

"Let's walk up the road and see my friend Bessie," I suggested.

David loved walks of any kind, so off we went. The farmhouse sat in the afternoon sun with no one around. David started to turn back, but I convinced him we should at least get a closer look at the place. I took four steps up to the porch and knocked on the door. I didn't expect anyone to answer because Bessie's truck was missing.

David gazed at the pasture and surrounding forest while I tried the back door. No one was home. Since I was already in the back yard, I decided to cut across about a hundred feet of grass and check out the barn. Up close, I realized how big it was—much bigger than the house.

I heard a whinny, then another.

The barn door swung open with an easy touch. The smell of hay put me quickly at ease, until I saw a gray pickup truck parked next to a small corral with two brown horses in it. They whinnied. Looking past the truck, I saw heaps of building materials. Was Brody in construction? If his truck was in the barn, where was he? I heard someone behind me and twirled around.

"Looking for someone?" a deep voice asked.

I looked up at a large man wearing camo shorts and a white grungy t-shirt, finally recognizing him as Bessie's nephew, Brody, from the picnic at Twin Lakes Beach.

My voice failed me at first. Finally I was able to tell the young man that I was looking for Bessie.

"You might be lookin' for Bessie, but you found Brody," he grinned a crooked grin and stepped closer to me. Out of the corner of my eye, I was looking for a place to run, but there wasn't one. I was backed up against the back bumper of his truck, and he and his breath were already too close for comfort.

"What happened to your head?" I asked, looking up at a good-size bandage taped to Brody's forehead. Even as I asked the question, pieces of the puzzle were falling into place.

"What's it to you?"

"Just wondering how you were getting along," I said, trying to act casual, as I recognized the garlic breath.

"To tell you the truth," he touched the tape with two fingers, "it hurts, but I'm alive. At the hospital they told me that two women pulled me out of the truck I was driving…and there were flames all around."

"Just in the grass," I corrected him.

He stared at me for a moment. "Don't tell me it was you!" His mouth dropped open and tears welled in his eyes. "Is your name, Josephine?"

"Yep, and Fiona and I pulled you out of the U-Drive…after you smashed her beautiful car!"

He looked confused, but stepped back a bit into a less threatening posture. "Josephine," his voice cracked. "I have no excuse for the way I acted, and I'm indebted to you for saving my life." He hung his head like a little boy in big trouble.

"Do you have a dog named, Thor?" his voice wavered.

"Yes and no, his name is actually Solow."

"You really had me goin' with that dog of yours."

"Brody, how deep are you into selling the construction materials?" I asked, starting to feel more confident and in control.

"I was just a delivery guy, until I got the idea of holding up the delivery and asking for more money. It worked pretty well until I went too far and asked for the woman's purse. But it would have worked if you hadn't come along."

"Who's your boss?"

"He'll kill me if I say...but I'll tell you anyway. The guy's name is Rodney Plodnick. I don't know where he lives. He calls me, and I pick up and deliver. A few days ago he told me and Chris and Ponce to rent three U-Drives and clean out Eddie's basement."

"Did he tell you why he wanted to empty out the basement...?" I asked, excited that I was finally getting closer to the truth.

"No, but your name came up a few times, along with a lot of cussing. I think he wanted to get rid of you once and for all. But I never thought he would burn down Eddie's house, knowing you were in it."

"Did you have any part in burning down Eddie's house?"

Brody stared at the dirt floor. "I've done some bad stuff, but I would never do that...you gotta believe me." His voice cracked.

"Thank you, Brody, for being honest with me. Do you know if Rod was in touch with Fiona Garrett?"

"The woman with the fancy red car?"

I nodded.

"Yeah, like I said, he was selling her some of his stuff for the homeless project."

"Looks like you're keeping some of Rod's stuff here in the back of the barn." My eyes went to the piles of hardware and such stacked against the far wall. "Same kind of things I saw in Eddie's basement."

I heard a door slam in the distance.

"Yeah, Rod's renting space from ME now," he laughed.

"So, how much does your Aunt Bessie know about this?" I asked, listening to footsteps coming toward the barn door.

"Not much. She knows I'm selling and delivering stuff—that's all."

The footsteps stopped.

I saw David escort Bessie into the barn.

A horse whinnied.

"Did you kill Eddie?" I asked.

Brody shook his head slowly, sadly.

Bessie stepped forward.

"He didn't kill nobody," she said.

"How do you know that," I asked.

"Because it was me that did it. I was loadin' up some firewood from Eddie's stack when he come home early, in a bad mood. He was so tight with his stuff, after us bein' friends for so many years. He was too cheap to let me have some wood and water, so I always took it when he was gone."

Brody hung his head, looking like he might cry.

"Well, he come home, and threatened me with his rifle he kept in the truck. Gave me a bad time, so I hauled off and hit him in the back of the head with a piece of firewood. He fell forward into the little stream of water. I was so mad I just got in my truck and drove home, figuring he'd pull himself out of the water…but he didn't." Her voice went down to a whisper, "I loved that man."

Epilogue

The Staley's were forever grateful to Josephine for all the lovely murals she and her cohorts had produced. But most of all for bringing home their beloved Herbert, who surprised everyone with a litter of four healthy kittens on the Fourth of July.

Nibs signed up for gambling therapy and was rehired by the Staleys on conditions of reimbursement. He gave up gambling, but Myrtle never even considered giving up her pension for poker.

Officers Sayer and Lund, working as a close-knit team, brought Rodney Plodnick in for questioning. It didn't go well for Rodney. He would have to go to trial for a hundred and thirty-two counts of theft, a hit-and-run, one count of arson and one count of conspiring to murder three women in a basement.

Sayer and Lund also arrested Bessie for second-degree murder. Her fate would be in the hands of a jury. Her nephew, Brody, had earned a twelve-month sentence in County Jail. Because he was so remorseful, he ended up serving only six months.

Fiona turned her life around, quit the City Council and concentrated on legal methods of helping the homeless. She and Jimmy could be spotted cruising around in their new but unpretentious mid-size Mazda SUV. They quietly donated the Lamborghini insurance money to the homeless project. Jimmy retired from IBM and began helping Fiona with her charity work, whenever they weren't traveling together.

Chester hired Chris and Ponce to help him with his building projects, teaching them good carpentry as they went along.

To Liana's delight, the Staley's Library was featured in the September issue of *Architectural Digest*, and the Chop Suey mural made it into the October issue.

Denise and Calvin took a Fourth of July weekend trip together to the wine country to celebrate the officers' working together again. There were fireworks!

David built and installed four owl houses on his property. The elegant birds moved in and took over David's gopher work so that he had more time to spend with Josephine.

THE END

ABOUT THE AUTHOR

Author Joyce Oroz is not only passionate about her writing, painting and large family, she loves being involved in her community. Aromas, California, is a very small town, perfect for working with friends and neighbors. Oroz' most recent endeavor was helping children paint their zucchinis—as in Squash, for the zucchini races at the Harvest Festival. She also has a real soft spot for the annual county fair and loves to bring that small-town flavor into her stories.

BOOKS BY AUTHOR JOYCE OROZ

The Josephine Stuart Mystery Series
Secure the Ranch
Read My Lipstick
Shaking In Her Flip Flops
Cuckoo Clock Caper
Beetles in the Boxcar
Roller Rubout
Scent of a $windle
Who Murdered Mary Christmas
Pushing Up Daisy
Hill Street Clues
Dead on a Rifle

Non-fiction
Muraling for Fun & Profit
Sena's Light

Children's Books
Annie Gets Her Bounce
Annie Gets a Brother
Grady Ghost Has a Secret—coming soon